Vindication Across Time

I0592543

MALA NAIDOO

ABOUT THE AUTHOR

Born in South Africa during the apartheid era, **Mala Naidoo** worked as a teacher of English literature in South Africa and Australia. She encourages young people to be 'moved' by reading and inspires confidence and compassion through creative expression. From a very young age, Mala was surrounded by books from the English literary canon. She also enjoys biographies, autobiographies and contemporary novels, and believes that a good dose of life experience and fiction has shaped the representation of places, events and characters in her writing.

Publisher: Mala Naidoo
website: malanaidoo.com

First published in Australia 2017
This edition published 2017
Copyright © Mala Naidoo 2017
Cover design, typesetting: WorkingType (www.workingtype.com.au)

Naidoo, Mala
Vindication Across Time
ISBN- 978-0-648-13770-2

pp208

With Gratitude To
My Ancestors

Chapter 1

These late eclipses in the sun and moon
portend no good to us.
Shakespeare — *King Lear*

~

The high-speed ambulance ride to the emergency department had Meryl in a silent daze. Visions of Andrei, motionless on the ground, bleeding from the head, flashed before her eyes, in the dazzling lights and blaring siren of the emergency vehicle that carried a man who was still a mystery to her. Ben and Michael discussed the gunshot to the head in lowered tones as the driver tried to keep pace with the ambulance.

Andrei's son, Alec, was to arrive from New York the next day to talk to Inspector Aldo in the hope that he would demystify why Professor Andrei Malakov, his father, was gunned down.

Ben promised to remain with Meryl in Florence until Andrei was in Alec's care.

*   *   *

Inspector Aldo paced the hospital corridor outside Andrei's room — pensive, tapping the side of his head with his right hand index finger and running his left hand through his hair with agitated energy as he made low sighing and grunting sounds.

The fog of the last twenty-four hours was dense... Meryl was on a literary junket, now here she was in the middle of an investigation of a man she knew very little about other than his literary prowess and impending divorce.

Michael walked around confused, drinking endless cups of coffee, stubble visible on his otherwise clean-shaven face, his eyes were bloodshot. He avoided eye contact with Meryl. Why did she insist on this trip without him? Why did she act so impulsively in taking up the offer to stay at Andrei's cottage in Viareggio? A thousand 'why's' cavorted in his mind leaving him tense and edgy, oblivious to the comings and goings along the hospital corridor.

Ben walked close to Meryl, she looked up at him with a tired, aged, helpless look. Her bright large, brown eyes were dull, her hair a mess of curls hanging about her shoulders. Andrei lay motionless, his head swathed in bandages; the oozing blood stain on the left side of his head had spread halfway across, to the right side.

Seven hours in surgery, with no sign of movement from Andrei after three hours in recovery, made Meryl more anxious with each passing hour. She sat at Andrei's bedside in ICU, waiting for him to say something... something to help her understand. Her hands trembled from too many cups of coffee which she drank to stay alert to avoid collapsing in an exhausted heap.

'Meryl,' Ben whispered, 'you should step outside a bit and get something to eat, I'm sure Alec will want some time alone with his father. Come with me Meryl, let's take a walk.' His gentle voice soothed her overwrought mind like a much-needed balm.

'You're right, I should allow Alec some privacy with Andrei.

It must be awful for him seeing his father this way among people he has never met before.'

In all the time that had elapsed since the shooting, she did not stop to think how Michael might be feeling, seeing her so infused by pain and grief over Andrei.

Inspector Aldo, now less agitated, pounced on Meryl as she stepped out the doorway of Andrei's hospital room.

'We need to talk Ms Moorecroft. I have a few questions to ask you, this is an official case and if Mr Malakov dies, we have a murder on our hands. This makes you, your fiancé, Michael Morrissey and Dr Hart suspects.'

She stared at him without absorbing his calculated, brutal comments. Ben jumped up with irritation in his voice,

'Inspector Aldo, under the circumstances can you please defer your questions to later, my niece needs to have something to eat and freshen herself up before she is in the right frame of mind to entertain your questions and please refrain from surmising the outcome of Professor Malakov's recovery.'

'Entertain my questions! Indeed! Dr Hart, I am cautioning you, this situation has escalated from your niece being *a missing person* to a possible homicide so choose your words wisely, your manner perturbs me, to say the least!'

Michael looked up when he heard Aldo's clenched, raised voice... He walked up to Ben and Meryl.

'Is everything okay Ben?'

'Yes, yes Michael, I was just telling the *good inspector* that Meryl needs to eat and freshen herself up before he can begin interrogating her.'

'Interrogating? What for?'

'Well,' Ben whispered, 'we will *all* be 'suspects' if poor Andrei does not pull through, more you and me as we were the first ones close up at the crime scene. I tell you, it feels like we are in some nightmarish dream and we will soon wake up safely in our beds.' His voice trailed off with emotional exhaustion. His quiet, sedate lifestyle was now churned inside out.

Meryl struggled to keep a morsel down, she picked at the chicken salad, gulped down her eighth coffee that day. She looked at Michael and Ben with a wrinkled brow that claimed her usual youthful look and cheerful disposition.

'I am so sorry to have put you both through this, it's my responsibility to see that Andrei is made comfortable as he recovers from this ordeal — please forgive me...' she reached out and squeezed both their hands, her large brown eyes brimmed with tears. 'Ben, you should return to London and Michael you cannot put your work on hold any longer, please go home as soon as you need to, it will be grossly unfair for me to expect you to stay on.'

Both remained silent.

Inspector Aldo pulled a chair and sat beside Meryl.

'Ms Moorecroft, do you have any idea who took you from the cottage at Viareggio?' His gnawing persistence was the final stroke for Ben,

'*Took her*, don't you mean forcibly kidnapped her, Inspector? Have you seen the scars around her wrists and ankles?'

'Mr Morrissey, I am appealing to you to speak to Dr Hart to refrain from interjecting with his unnecessary remarks when I am *not* addressing him!' Inspector Aldo's vocal irritation attracted the attention of people in the cafeteria who looked at the three of them with suspicion.

'Ben,' Michael whispered, 'let's get out of here for a while.'

Ben reluctantly followed Michael out, shooting the inspector an irritated backward glance.

'Inspector, I don't know who took me from the house but I know who held me captive, he said he was Andrei's son, while

4

I know it's not appropriate to ask Alec any questions just yet, he will be able to clarify his brother's relationship with their father. Although based on no solid evidence other than my intuition, the person who served me meals while I was held hostage, appeared to be Andrei's housekeeper.

'We cannot go on your intuitions Ms Moorecroft, I need hard, cold facts. I will speak to Alec soon to shed light on his mysterious father. This seems an unnecessary mess that you have got yourself into, Mr Morrissey seems a sensible man, Dr Hart, I suspect will do anything for you, no doubt. The question is would he be prepared to kill for you?'

Meryl's jaw dropped in disbelief at this horrible insinuation that crossed all boundaries of professional ethics and levelled a horrendous assumption about her beloved Ben.

'I take exception, Inspector, to your incriminating suppositions! Ben will not harm a fly and will be most distressed should he know that you are looking at him as a suspect in Andrei's attack. He is a respected physician in London and my much-loved relative.'

'Well, as Shakespeare said, *Time shall unfold what plighted cunning hides.* Indeed, I may not appear to be a Shakespearean scholar, nor *Mr Darcy*, I certainly do my homework on my suspects.' He stood up quite suddenly, looked down at Meryl and smiled, 'have a good night Ms Moorecroft, I would not leave the country if I were you.'

He walked away, head bent, and shoulders stooped with a noticeable dragging of his left foot, Meryl stood staring after him for a few seconds before she walked into Andrei's room where Alec sat gently stroking his father's hands.

She sat beside him looking at Andrei. He was pale, with a grey, ghostly tinge visible in his cheeks.

Alec's sad smile asked a million questions — the time was not right now — he needed to talk to Meryl about the days leading up to his father's departure to Moscow.

The mystery of Professor Andrei Malakov lay locked in his comatose world.

Chapter 2

Who with best meaning have incurr'd the worst...?
Shakespeare — King Lear

~

Michael left Meryl in Florence.

Marcia coped well on her own with her new position, Ted and answering all Michael's emails and telephone calls. They had to finalise the amendment to workplace harassment which was to be tabled at the Human Rights Commission sitting before it was tabled in parliament.

Michael was happy to have Marcia pick him up from the airport and settle down to a quiet dinner after the emotionally draining days in Florence.

Ted nuzzled up to Marcia, curling around her feet, glancing up at her in brown-eyed adoration.

'Hey Teddo! What's up guy? Forgot me already? What will you do when Meryl returns?'

Ted snorted and recircled his position around Marcia's feet, moving his head around into a comfortable spot between both her feet as he fell into a blissful sleep oblivious to Michael's presence in the room.

'How are things with Meryl's friend, any improvement to

his condition before you left?' She asked with sensible caution aware that the past two weeks were telling on a leaner looking Michael before her.

'He's still in a clinically induced coma, the blood clot on his brain, caused by the bleeding, is inoperable at the moment. The bullet has to be removed. The danger is, if proceeded with, there is no guarantee that he will be able to speak nor walk again. The swelling in the brain has not subsided as expected.'

'How is Meryl holding up, Michael?'

'Thank you for asking, honestly, I think she has no idea what she has let herself in for in forming this relationship... friendship. Poor Ben, he loves Meryl to distraction and will stand by her like a rock.'

'You should go back Michael to see her through this you know, she will need more support now more than ever.'

'Look, I will only go back if things get messy for her, right now she appears in control and Andrei's son, Alec arrived from New York. He is depending on her to see him through this time. I would be the third wheel, serving no purpose other than as bystander.'

'You know what's best.'

'I hope so, I just wish this mess could have been averted. Inspector Aldo is so cagey, I'm surprised he didn't insist I stay on, he is highly suspicious of the three of us in this matter.'

'You, Meryl and Alec?'

'No, not Alec, but poor Ben.'

'Really?'

'It appears Professor Malakov was under the watchful eye of the police in Florence for his wild parties and odd working pattern. They have nothing on him... well for now it appears. Who knows what else will emerge in the days ahead.'

'Hopefully, he will recover soon and Meryl can return home, I'm sure she must want to be back here.'

'Not sure, really, so much has changed. It appears that she had a rough time when she was held in that remote villa, she indicated that she thought the housekeeper was also involved. Andrei's older son is a suspect too, so Aldo is going to reel him in apparently.'

'I suppose then there will be a trial soon.'

'Let's put that to rest now. Tell me now, what have you been getting up to apart from helping me so much.'

'I've been so comfortable here and it's been peaceful too. I will stay tonight but will have to go back to my apartment tomorrow, to allow you time to get on with your work.'

'You don't have to Marcia, I'm happy to have you stay on as long as you want.'

'That's really kind of you, but, I should get back tomorrow.'

The conversation drifted to South Africa and the plans Marcia had for going back for a visit. She planned to go over in a few months when her teaching block ended at the International School. She invited Michael to join her on this trip.

'How do you know the school won't ask you to stay on?'

'It's a long service leave position that I'm filling in now. If more blocks come up, I will certainly consider it. I'm afraid to commit to anything long-term after my last experience. I'm content with this for now, that I have a job where the colour of my skin is not the discriminator for my ability and skills. I have to save for a rainy day too.'

'I do understand what you mean. Remember never let fear guide the value you have both as a person and professional.'

'Thank you Michael, the scars are still there, just below the surface, five years was a long time to eat, sleep and dread the next crushing comment. My sleep pattern is still erratic. Time, I suppose will heal the wound, I hope …'

'Hang in there, I have great faith in that you won't be leaving this country in any permanent way.'

Michael rose to comfort Marcia with an embrace that he needed more than she did, when he was interrupted by the ringing landline.

'Hi Mum, yes I'm back safe and sound, how have you been?' Angela was concerned about Michael's emotional state, she said the television news had reported the situation regarding Meryl and Andrei in Florence almost nightly since his departure.

'Yes, I'm well, nothing to worry about, Meryl stayed on to see things through. He laughed when she asked if 'the nice South African lady' was going to continue helping him with Ted. Her anxiety escalated in recent months as Alzheimer's started to take seed.

*   *   *

He was happy to be home but felt the weight of the world with Meryl's situation. She was reluctant to speak about her ordeal leading up to Andrei being shot. He knew Inspector Aldo would not leave any stone unturned when he hounded her for the details of her encounter with Andrei Malakov, the night of her abduction and the days thereafter. He knew she valued her privacy, being asked to recount intimate details in a public forum would test her. All he hoped for now was that she had the mental capacity to cope.

He looked around the house which was a shrine of her books, shoes, dresses and other holiday memorabilia. He found it difficult to shut out thoughts of her. He could not blame Marcia for wanting to return to her apartment. Who would want to be with a man who was not present in every moment they spent together? He lay in bed thinking about her humanitarian contribution which was close to being finalised. Her charismatic personality and graceful beauty, her commitment to and passion for her work made her a desirable catch. He mulled over why she had not formed any romantic liaisons in the last five years.

He fell asleep reliving his boyhood days when things were simpler and uncomplicated.

*   *   *

Michael jumped out of bed to the aromatic smell of coffee brewing. Marcia was humming as she prepared breakfast.

'Good morning Mr Morrissey! Did you sleep well, I hope you're ravenous. I've prepared a hearty breakfast.'

'Look at you, Ms Ntuli, the perfect housewife! What time did you get up?'

'I've been up since 5:30 am, I have to attend a conference which is a re-run of the one I missed earlier this month. I have my bags packed. I'll leave after breakfast and call you tomorrow night.'

Michael felt a tinge of sadness creep over him. Marcia was eager to be gone, out of his home and he feared, out of his life. He had no right to expect her to put him first. He did not want to appear clingy. He cringed remembering Meryl's accusations about his neediness throughout their years together.

'Will you come over tomorrow? We can chat about the news that has come through from the Human Rights Commission.'

'No Michael, you need to rest, I'll ring you tomorrow and perhaps see you next weekend.'

'Next weekend! Why not during the ...?' He stopped and remained silent for a brief second as he made a mental note to stop appearing needy if he hoped to keep Marcia close.

'You need the time too, to mull over all that has happened. You should check in on Meryl. I will call you to arrange a meeting again.'

Deep down he felt Marcia was making her exit but was too polite to say so in explicit terms. He knew that the situation with Meryl had made her reassess the spontaneous 'relationship' that started before he was interrupted by Meryl's disappearance in Florence.

He accepted that perhaps she was right, he needed time to think, to absorb all that transpired in the last ten days.

How could he expect her to play second fiddle to Meryl?

Chapter 3

O damn'd Iago! O inhuman dog!
Shakespeare — Hamlet

~

Andrei's condition was no different. Meryl and Alec remained at his bedside night and day alternating nights to ensure they both had adequate rest. Ben spent some of the days with Meryl at the hospital retreating to his hotel each afternoon. She was aware that this endless waiting for a sign of Andrei's recovery was making Ben weary. Her appeals to him to return to London fell on deaf ears, he was adamant that they would return together.

Inspector Aldo was a restless beast as he grew impatient with each passing day. After almost four hours with Alec at the police station he told Meryl he had to see her the next day at 9 am for a round of questions on how she met, Professor Andrei Malakov and any matter she could shed light on regarding his shooting. This left Meryl nervous and agitated as she paced the hospital floor on her night vigil.

'Andrei, do you hear me? Press my hand if you hear me.'

Andrei lay motionless, his face grew thinner day by day. She sat staring at him, he appeared so small under the starched covers. He looked somewhat taller, lying flat on his back, wired through from head to neck like a Frankenstein project. His chalk-white, parted lips were dry, a little blue and beginning to crack. She reached over and applied lip balm to them.

'I'm not sure why this has happened, Alec is here with me, thankfully. We will not rest until we know what happened on that fateful night. I miss hearing you call me *'moya zvezda'* and can't wait to speak to you again, please fight this, come back to us, Alec needs you Andrei and... so do... I, please.'

* * *

Meryl arrived at police headquarters the next morning while Alec watched over Andrei.

'Good morning Ms Moorecroft, bright and early I see, eager to begin?'

She was beginning to get accustomed to the inspector's cynical tone and caustic comments. What she wondered was whether it was his professional or personal persona that came across. She had never had any reason in her forty years to be involved with the police, least of all in Florence, so far away from home.

'Would you like coffee before we commence or tea that you English prefer?'

'I'm not English, Inspector Aldo, coffee would be lovely, thank you.'

She knew she had to keep her composure as Inspector Aldo had cast suspicion in her direction.

'Well, Dr Hart, your uncle, is quite the English gentleman, except when he is angered, so I assumed, as his niece, you might be too.'

'Ben is not English by birth, he has lived in England since he was eighteen so that is as English as he is. He is a dignified man, standing tall among those who cannot hold a candle to him.' Her dagger was uttered with pointed intention.

'Yes, yes, I get it Ms Moorecroft. I must be mindful not to say anything that might be construed as uncomplimentary to Dr Hart, right?' That sardonic grin irked her.

'May we proceed with what it is you wish to ask me Inspector Aldo?'

'Let's begin. How long have you known Professor Malakov and how did you meet? This is official, I am recording your responses, Ms Moorecroft so please be direct.'

'Three or four months, I was on tour in Bath and he approached me to borrow a chair from my table at the local tea shop as there were many members in his group.'

'Three or four? Which one is it, four is four weeks more than three months and a lot can happen in four weeks, be *specific* Ms Moorecroft, how long have you known the professor?'

'It's four months, well four months on Monday.'

'Mmm, good, now who were these people he was with?'

'I did not meet them on the first encounter. I assumed they were a literary group travelling for a common purpose.'

'Did not meet them on the first encounter... I see... so when did you meet them again?'

'A few of them were present at the opera we attended in London a few weeks... two weeks after we met in Bath.'

'Are you saying you swapped telephone numbers at the tea shop, *in a matter of minutes?*'

'No Inspector Aldo, that is not what happened, I met Andrei on the bus later that day, he sat next me as no other seats were available and we got chatting. This was when I realised he was a professor of English literature, a visiting lecturer at universities across England. As we shared an interest in this area we thought we would communicate with each other thereafter.'

'Aah, so you are an English professor too?'

'No, I am pursuing a writing career after being an editor for some time hence my visit to England.'

'So, England, is it a writer's paradise Ms Moorecroft?'

'I draw inspiration from being in England. Ben has inspired me since I was a child.'

'Quite smitten with Dr Hart, I see,' his jeering laugh made her want to yell at him to stop his insane, crass comments.

'Is there a problem with that sir?' Meryl could not contain this outburst any longer. Inspector Aldo was deliberately pressing all the wrong buttons.

'No offence or insult intended, my dear Ms Moorecroft, you do understand I have to piece together how you got yourself into this mess.'

'Mess? I did not create any of this and I am a victim of a situation I do not understand.'

'Oh, Professor Malakov was mysterious then, he did not tell you much about his personal life, did he?'

'In the brief time we spent together at Viareggio, he talked about his impending divorce and his struggles with Mariya's, his estranged wife's family. This is Alec Malakov's mother that I refer to.'

'Yes, Malakov junior said as much yesterday without too many details. Why were you left alone in the cottage in Viareggio when Professor Malakov fled to Moscow?'

'Firstly, he did not *flee*, he informed me he was requested to be in Moscow to finalise his divorce, he did not leave me alone; Ana, the housekeeper and Dmitri the driver were at my disposal as arranged by Andrei.'

'So are you saying the housekeeper and driver were on the premises when you were abducted?'

'No, they left that morning, in fact Dmitri, the driver was not staying at the cottage, he came in from the city to take Ana back to town for a few days, I assume she realised that I did not need much care and was quite self-sufficient.'

'Not quite though, if you were 'abducted' Ms Moorecroft.' The daft twinkle in his eye made Meryl decidedly uncomfortable, she felt the sweat prickle on her neck again as her heart quickened making her feel faint. She did not have breakfast that morning compounded by the nervous energy that kept her up all night and now the infuriating questioning by Inspector Aldo escalated her defence and attack mode, sapping all her energy. Her fear intensified with thoughts of what might be revealed about Andrei that she was not quite ready to hear.

'That's a little unfair, sir, considering I was not prepared for any of this.'

'How did you explain all of this to Mr Morrissey, your fiancé, I gather?'

'This does not seem to be a question that will lead to finding the people who took me from the house or those who shot Andrei.'

'Aha! You seem to think they are not one and the same. What are you withholding Ms Moorecroft?'

'While I was being held captive, one of the voices indicated that Andrei was his father, I'm not sure if this is true and have not broached this with Alec as we have met for the first time in recent days.'

'Very interesting indeed! This gets more complicated with each question I ask.' He looked at Meryl with a penetrating stare, his eyes then roved across her face and down to her neck.

What could he be thinking her involvement was in all of this? How was she going to explain this hideous interview to Ben? How did she end up in such a situation? Her intentions had been good and here she was sitting in a police station under the scrutiny of Inspector Aldo who thought she was a foolish woman who trusted a foreigner on a whim or that she might be involved in the criminal activities being investigated.

'Ms Moorecroft, since you are a writer, or should I say, 'hopeful writer', please write a report on the night you were taken and the three days thereafter. Do not embellish anything! This is not Agatha Christie's crime fiction *Miss Marple*, oops sorry, Ms Moorecroft so keep to the facts. You writers and your wild imaginations can complicate things for people like me. Hard core facts please.'

Meryl breathed a sigh of relief that this ordeal was over. She cringed from the '*hopeful writer*,' '*Miss Marple*' and '*wild imaginations*' comments and agreed to write a report as requested. She politely thanked the inspector and left.

Chapter 4

It is a wise father that knows his own child.
Shakespeare — *The Merchant of Venice*

~

Ben waited for Meryl in the foyer of their hotel, staring ahead without seeing her come through the doors.

'Hello there, how are you today?'

'Agitated to say the least, Meryl. I was on tenterhooks all day wondering how things were going with Inspector Aldo. Did you stop at the hospital after the 'interrogation?'

'I knew you would be worried so I hurried back to you. Alec is at the hospital and will call me should there be any change with Andrei. I'll have a nap and take over from Alec later.'

'Why do you have to be there either all day or all night? You barely knew the man, Meryl.'

Meryl was silent, not knowing how to respond to what in essence was the truth. How was she ever going to tell Ben, she had given her heart to this mysterious, 'roving professor?' He would not believe that she was so far into a relationship that had barely got off the ground and showed all signs of being a dangerous liaison.

'I let my heart take over when I saw how helpless Alec looked.

We are both in the same situation with not having a clue as to what or why this has happened.'

'Alec too, is a stranger to you. I don't understand why you would risk everything after all that has happened, you should try to extricate yourself from this.'

'I know, I know Ben... please trust that this feels right to me... please allow me...,' she broke off not knowing what else to say, her eyes pleading, begging for understanding.

'How did things go with that *infernal* inspector?'

'He is a piece of work for sure, his insinuations angered me so much. I had to keep calm, it was difficult to listen to his relentless crude insults and assumptions.'

'Did you explain everything to him now?'

'Not everything, I have yet to tell him more on my suspicions regarding Ana's involvement. He referred to my 'wild imagination' and 'hopeful writer' status. I felt like a swatted fly, too weak and afraid to retaliate.'

'Incorrigible swine! We have to stand up for our innocence and stop him dead in his tracks when he makes such comments. What will you tell him about the housekeeper?'

'Ana was odd when she arrived at the cottage at Viareggio compared to her somewhat genial, though trite and officious manner at the apartment in the city.'

'What about the chauffeur, do you have any inkling whether he might be involved?'

'He was a man of few words. He displayed a deep almost servile manner in his respect for Andrei. I caught him trying to 'look' through the curtains in my bedroom upstairs when he came to take Ana back to the city after Andrei left for Moscow.'

'God heavens Meryl! You did not think to mention this to me earlier! Have you told Aldo?'

'No, we did not get that far. He will want to talk to me again.

Dmitri would not have been able to look into my bedroom, it was just odd that he was staring up at the window. He was pleasant enough and apologised for coming over so early. The one nagging thought I have is that I sent him a text message when I realised there were intruders in the house — he did not respond. Andrei told me to contact Dmitri if I needed anything that I could not take care of on my own.'

'It smells even more rotten, each time I hear more details. Go on.'

'I am fully aware that I have to let the inspector know that I contacted Dmitri. He must know this already seeing that Andrei was on the police radar here, as per the inspector. He won't elaborate on this for some reason.'

Ben shook his head in disbelief for the hundredth time, his furrowed frown had burrowed into a permanent fixture escalating the years, compounded by the sleepless nights of the last few weeks.

'I sincerely wish we could turn back the clock to a time that has erased this 'roving professor' from our lives. You are so deeply enmeshed in this that I fear it will be a long time before our lives are *normal* again.'

'Oh Ben, you have been negative ever since Andrei appeared, who knew this was going to happen?'

'It's better to err on the side of caution, taking it slow and easy, you did rush things a bit with coming over to Florence when he invited you.'

'No time for recriminations now, I have to keep a clear head to remember all that has happened.'

'I am just a caring, doting old fool, I'm sorry if I annoy you at times.'

'I need a reality check every now and then, you *do not* annoy me. I'm on a short fuse after the morning with Inspector Aldo.'

I'm heading off to the hospital in a few hours. Would you like to grab a quick lunch with me?'

The table they sat at was in the middle row of the restaurant. At a table to their left, quite close up, in this tiny, six seater restaurant, right up against the wall, sat two well-dressed men who appeared to be in their forties. They glanced up at Meryl and Ben and continued with their conversation which Meryl overheard in this tight space. The man with dark hair was heard saying,

'Terrible business up at the cottage in Viareggio, did you hear about it?'

The other replied, 'Which cottage?'

'The one with the olive grove.'

'Andrei Malakov's place?'

'Yes, you remember we went there for a New Year's Eve party in 2007, when Jenny was studying literature at the university. Professor Malakov invited Jenny to bring two guests along with her. Quite a place, quite a party!'

'What's happened there, I've been away and too tired to watch any news since I got back?'

Meryl nudged Ben and rolled her eyes with a slight tilt of the head in the direction of the men. Ben who was a little hard of hearing, knew Meryl's sign language very well. He tried to listen in, catching a few phrases.

'... a woman was taken from the house... not sure... the place is cordoned off by police now...'

Meryl strained to catch more of this conversation,

'*Seems like Andrei Malakov has not been up to any good, mixed up in some business I think. Albert said he saw him in Pelago about a month ago, wonder what he was doing there.*'

'*I wonder why such a city man, hot-shot professor would go to Pelago?*'

'Well, it can be secluded enough for anything he might want to conceal.'

'He has managed to keep above the law here although it's no secret that he is watched quite closely, Jenny's brother works in the police force and one night he revealed a little about the professor after one too many drinks...'

Meryl felt the hair on her body prickle, her appetite was killed with that last comment. She stared at the prawn linguini floating in the bowl. Ben picked at his food as they sat in ear shattering silence, craning to hear more.

They walked out onto the hotel patio leaving behind their unfinished lunch.

'Ben! Did you catch any of that? Local impressions of Andrei seem to suggest... he... might have been involved in something.'

'I'm afraid I only caught something about a woman being taken... you of course. Meryl, this is gossip now, we are not sure about anything at this stage. I think the older son holds the key to this mystery.'

Chapter 5

*Let us not burden our remembrances with a
heaviness that's gone –*
Shakespeare — The Tempest

~

M ichael and Marcia ploughed through documents on
the 1958 Employment and Occupation convention in
Geneva through to the 1964 Civil Rights Act and later. They
had opted to work more at Michael's place in recent weeks with
Marcia determined that she would go home each evening. They
spent some weekends ensuring that all the documents that were
to be submitted to the Human Rights Commission had no loop-
holes in their argument for changes on workplace harassment.

Michael tapped into Marcia's voices and visions of her days
under the apartheid regime.

'What was it like going into the city as a child and adult in
South Africa, Marcia?'

'The Group Areas Act meant that people lived in ethnic and
racially divided parts of town. The more affluent, so-called
white suburbs had park-like gardens, wider streets, paved sidewalks and supermarkets that stocked luxuries that downtown
black inhabited areas did not have. The streets on the other side

of town had stagnant water sitting in mosquito-infested gutters, unpaved sidewalks with people hawking their wares on street corners. The difference between the two was like being in two countries at the same time.'

'I find the Group Areas Act such a strategic divisive aspect of the apartheid era. Keeping people separated from each other's values and ways of thinking and living is loaded with power agendas — the very centre of Afrikaner thinker under Verwoerd.'

'I have nothing against the Afrikaner, it's the law that was so malicious and unjust. It was perceived as being instituted by the Afrikaner, but, hating the Afrikaners is a perpetuation or a reversal of apartheid. Senseless, to say the least. Many Afrikaners were unhappy with the lot of the black people and marched beside them in demonstrations that always resulted in violence. Trigger happy police instigated violence; they saw black people as objects rather than people.'

'Did you attend any gatherings where Nelson Mandela addressed the people?'

'Yes, I did, he visited many regional areas after his release from prison and I attended with my family. Just seeing his smiling face enter the community hall that was packed to the rafters is an experience I will never forget, the cheers from the crowd thundered through the room, rising to the roof with euphoria that I have never felt again with this magnitude. He was quite tall, an erect figure with a heart that brought sunshine to the darkest areas where poverty, hardship and a yearning for education reigned.'

'It certainly sounds like a spiritual moment. Please go on.'

'A few of us followed him around the country to other centres which were equally enthralled by his presence but the most memorable for me was at the foothills of the Drakensberg where his spirit was evocative, almost spiritual, here so close to nature. He loved chatting to young people during these tours, I attended the Drakensberg session with my cousin Uzoma, a lawyer who was lucky to get a moment to speak to Madiba who was always keen to talk to young lawyers. You will enjoy this Michael, he looked at Uzoma who was standing to his right when he asked,

'What is your name young man and which firm do you work for?'

My cousin replied, 'Uzoma Mkhize,' he was so nervous he forgot to add which firm he worked for and Madiba asked again,'

'Uzo, which firm do you work for?'

Referring to him as 'Uzo' with such familiarity made my cousin, who beamed from ear to ear, more comfortable to continue the conversation with Madiba.

Nelson Mandela smiled his characteristic radiant smile, the twinkle in his eye had everyone hanging onto his next word; he spoke with a quieter tone, although still smiling,

'Lawyers...mmm, I see, so different now to when I was a young man doing what you do, no fancy cars and Armani suits, very different indeed.' He laughed, 'don't look so serious Uzo, smile. Lawyers are too serious.'

Marcia continued, 'Everybody listened intently to every syllable uttered– he endured so much yet he smiled with such warmth and made a joke or two to erase fear and make all feel comfortable.'

'What an electrifying moment and certainly a memorable part of life this will always be,' Michael insisted on hearing more about Marcia's visions.

'Prior to Nelson Mandela's release, some activists joined forces with the police as *impimpis* which means informer or 'snitch.' They would do anything for a piece of bread. This created distrust amongst families and friends when they saw others with a little more than they had. The provocative question to those who were suspected as dissidents to the cause was, 'Hey *wena*, you *impimpi*?' Animosity was rife when poverty bred envy and crime took hold. Many young men suspected of being an *impimpi* were brutally murdered by their own people while activists were brutalised by the special branch of the police force. Sadly, some young men were innocently labelled as *impimpi* for a plate of food.'

'It must have been a horrible time that saw no reprieve from the injustice that apartheid created. Did you know any persons that were killed in detention?'

'Not first-hand although many of my friends' brothers, fathers and uncles were taken into custody after breaking the state of emergency law which you might know was that no gatherings on city streets were allowed as they were deemed to be meetings that could be planning to sabotage the Afrikaner government.'

Michael listened on to these true-life accounts of growing up in South Africa, he was silent throughout Marcia's recount.

'Do you have more questions, Michael?'

'What were your student days like?'

'We were forced to go to ethnic universities, unless we could provide medical reasons for why we could not attend the stipulated ethnic university. I refused to apply for concession to attend the local university so I had to live in the hostel at the university in the next town. It was a hot-bed of revolutionary political thought. Lots of meetings were held on the campus to ignite change, it was a passionate time in the cry for democracy.'

'What happened if someone did not want to be part of the resistance movement on campus?' Michael asked with grave consternation, his eyes fixed on Marcia's face as she recounted graphic details of racial strife.

'Sadly, they had to conform, there was no option, or they would be considered to be an *impimpi* — nobody would want such a label when passions were running high for freedom and democracy. You had to toe the line if you valued your safety. Those who were reluctant to join the movement were far and few between. Nobody would want to be ostracised from the student body especially when living in the campus residence. I saw many of the films, which were prohibited in South Africa, on Nelson Mandela's time in prison on Robben Island. The same films were viewed in the village where I grew up. Late night screenings were held in the local hall. Awareness filtered this way into communities as television had not been introduced in South Africa then. Keep the masses down through keeping them in the dark. Yes, this was very much the mood and tone in apartheid South Africa.'

'How does one remain intact through all of this? I find this unfathomable.'

'So, you think, I'm intact?' Marcia laughed.

'You know what I mean, I would have been a snivelling mess with all this going on in my world.'

'You learn to be resilient, to survive when you know you are capable of making worthy contribution to the world, you fight it when you have nothing to lose and so much to gain.'

Chapter 6

Now is the winter of our discontent
Shakespeare — Richard III

~

Andrei's condition deteriorated.

He was back in Intensive Care.

Doctors had grave concerns whether he would pull through.

Andrei's son, Boris who allegedly held Meryl hostage had not made an appearance.

This turn in Andrei's condition agitated Inspector Aldo who demanded more information in his investigation on the days Meryl was held captive.

She walked down to the Police Headquarters where Inspector Aldo waited in restless anticipation for her. He informed her it could take half a day to get through what he needed to know.

'How are things Ms Moorecroft?'

'I'm very concerned about Andrei's condition Inspector.'

'Well, we have to get on with the business of the investigation as this deterioration in Professor Malakov's condition creates urgency for answers. What specifically did the doctor say was the situation with him now?'

'Dr Spartan said it was a mild heart attack which might have been a reaction to the medication. Alec is not aware if his father has any allergies to any of the medications he is currently on. His son, Boris, is unreachable as you know. Alec has tried all possible contacts with no luck in sight. Andrei's ex-wife, that is if the marriage is now legally annulled, is ill and cannot make comment. That leaves me, a virtual stranger in his life; I am useless in this investigation, so you can understand the stress this has generated.'

'I am sure you feel immense pressure, Ms Moorecroft, but as I said, its business as usual here at HQ — the perpetrators need to be apprehended and a trial started before Professor Malakov departs this earthly plane. I don't mean to be a fatalist but this is the reality in my line of work. Shall we begin?'

Meryl was not in the least surprised at the inspector's callous attitude.

'Yes, yes, go ahead Inspector.'

'Do you have the report I asked you to write regarding the night you were taken and the three days thereafter?'

'I do sir, here it is.'

'Ahem! I see it's a bound copy, a novella of sorts,' that sardonic laugh resurfaced making Meryl's skin crawl.

He flicked through the report and asked Meryl to highlight what she deemed significant on her three days of captivity.

'The three things that do trouble me are Andrei's two employees, Ana the housekeeper and Dmitri his chauffeur. Ana was pleasant enough when I arrived at the apartment in Florence, she seemed a tad hostile after Andrei left for Moscow. It felt as if she did not want to be bothered with small talk and was there to merely serve meals and clean up. I put it down to culture or personality or perhaps what Andrei might have expected. Dmitri was exceptionally quiet, but not really odd, except when it appeared he was trying to 'observe' my movements in the upstairs bedroom. He was staring up at my window from the backyard which made me feel uncomfortable enough to slip out of view. I sent him a text message, which you can see on my phone, the night I knew there were intruders in the house. He did not reply to my call for help. Andrei told me to contact Dmitri should I need anything while he was away. I also thought the hooded female figure that served me meals during my captivity appeared to be Ana. I judged this from her hands which were exposed — she served me meals at the cottage at Viareggio, serving and clearing up after me made her hands most visible to me every day, she never stayed around to chat, she was always in a hurry so her hands are remembered instead of any conversation we might have had. She chose to remain distant in a 'serving role' which did not make me feel very comfortable as, it's not something I'm used to.' Meryl had played this out in her mind a million times. She spoke with computerised precision.

She looked at Inspector Aldo who listened like an unmoving mountain, his unflinching stare made her feel naked, exposed to his strange, random mood shifts. She cleared her throat and continued.

'The other matter that somewhat perturbs me, as I cannot verify it, is that one of my captors, a very well-spoken male, that is, well-spoken in English indicated he was Andrei's son. He informed me that I would have to speak to Andrei and tell him what the demand was for my release. It was a very brief call as telecommunications will reveal in your investigation. A gunman with a rifle stood over me during the ransom call. None of this makes any sense. The voice I heard in the house rummaging through Andrei's study in Viareggio sounded similar to the voice of his 'son'. These are the most significant recollections that are worth reiterating. The captors who transported me to the place where I was held, sounded different to those who held me hostage at the location where I was found. I hope this makes sense, Inspector.'

'Thank you Ms Moorecroft, thank you for your detailed recount, however none of these can be verified as you were in an area with no natural or artificial light and you indicted that the assailants were hooded, just human shapes or blobs in the darkness. We have to track Professor Malakov's son, Boris, if he is indeed the one that held you captive. That too, is based on your speculation. We might get you to listen in to an interview with him to assess whether it was truly him that held you. As for the housekeeper and the driver, they too, have to be found and brought in. We shall have to find more details on them as I assume you do not know their last names, is that correct?'

'That is correct, sir, my time with them was brief and formal so I am unable to provide any further information. Is there anything more that you require from me?'

'What was Professor Malakov's relationship with his younger son Alec? Did he divulge much in the brief time you both spent together?'

'He seemed fond of Alec who he described as his 'arty boy', saying his older son was close to his mother and grandfather and that he had a few brush ups with the law in Russia.'

'So, he *did* say a lot to you about his private life! Interesting, although he appeared to be a very private, insular man. He is a parent who plays favourites with his children too. A strange lot indeed, this Malakov family — Professor Malakov was under our watchful eye because of his Russian connection. No doubt, much will be revealed, once all offending parties are at a trial to clear this up. I will let you go now Ms Moorecroft but remember you have to stay in town.'

Meryl had hoped that what she saw as a hint of 'softening'

in the Inspector's attitude towards her would last. His sinister warning made her realise she was not off his 'suspicious' list.

'Yes, Inspector I am aware that I cannot leave town.'

The gnawing thought that niggled Meryl was that Inspector Aldo seemed to have a personal disdain for Andrei that did not make sense in his professional capacity as an investigating inspector. He made many, unfounded personal judgements that did not sit well with her.

*　　*　　*

Meryl headed back to the hotel to fill Ben in on her second meeting with the inspector. There was no answer when she knocked on his door. She rang his mobile phone which he picked up on the second ring sounding a little breathless.

'Ben where are you?'

'Oh hello, you're back already, has something happened? I decided to talk a stroll on the Ponte Vecchio as it's a lovely morning, I'm heading back to the hotel now, meet me downstairs.'

'No, nothing different from what we already know. See you soon.'

She was relieved that Ben was out and about and getting some air and sunshine. He had remained cooped up in the hotel ever since Michael left Florence.

He walked in with a rosy glow appearing far more energetic than he had been of late.

'You look like you enjoyed the walk Ben, that's good to see.'

'Yes, I feel quite energised after that brisk walk! Did the inspector behave himself today, was he able to curb his caustic tongue?'

'Mercurial, to say the least. There was a point when I thought we had turned a corner when he seemed to trust my recollections of my time with Andrei and his staff and just as suddenly he told me, as an unmistakable warning, I was not to leave town. He gives me the shivers.'

'Yes 'mercurial' describes him to a 'T'. I suppose we have to sit tight and hope Andrei pulls through soon to stop these suspicions cast on us — Andrei will clear that up once he's well again.'

'Hopefully that will be soon. I cannot imagine how Alec feels about all that is going on.'

Ben suddenly grabbed Meryl's arm as he pointed at the television screen in the hotel reception area. The sound was barely audible with the checking in and checking out of people who felt the need to bid endless loud *arrivederci's* to staff as they departed.

On the screen flashed images of Ana, Dmitri and a male figure who Meryl assumed was Boris Malakov which was confirmed when their names appeared under each photograph. The public was urged to call crime-stoppers as a matter of urgency should they know the whereabouts of any of these persons of interest.

Meryl stared at the television, her large brown eyes now saucers — it was unbelievable how quickly Inspector Aldo had got this all-points bulletin circulating. He must have tremendous influence on the political and media fronts.

Inspector Aldo was a dark horse. She wanted to avoid too many interactions with him. His slow, lingering, travelling eyes, resting in a leering stare on her chest made her cringe. Had she become so accustomed to Ben's open and honest manner that she might be overreacting to the inspector's roving eyes? These thoughts were hard to shake. She figured he would be any woman's worst nightmare with his arrogance, demands and put downs.

Chapter 7

There's a special providence in the fall of a sparrow.
Shakespeare — Hamlet

~

Alec was frazzled when Meryl arrived at the hospital that afternoon. Andrei was now on life support. He had no family to turn to. Andrei was his anchor — the only one who understood his creative, sensitive and dreamy personality.

'You should have called Alec, I would have got here sooner.'

'I did not want to disturb you with this news while you were with Inspector Aldo, I knew your hours with him would have left you depleted. I do hope Boris turns up soon — not that he will be of any assistance in this situation. I am truly grateful that you have remained with papa, this is far more than I can bear alone.'

'I need to know that Andrei will be well again if I choose to leave. Inspector Aldo has also indicated that a trial will be in motion soon... if... Andrei...,' she broke off, unable to utter the harsh truth to this gentle soul who rushed to be at its father's bedside and who was as vulnerable as a little boy watching his father fading.

'Andrei spoke of you when he called me while he was in England, he said he met a woman who could have been all he needed and desired in his life and that he wished that he had met you at the beginning... years ago,'

'Thank you for sharing that with me, you do know that we had... er... have... a platonic friendship... mutual respect based on our love of literature.'

'Oh yes, Andrei was clear that you were not out for anything other than professional friendship... he said... what does it matter now, let's hope he can tell you what he feels so deeply...'

Meryl sat with bowed head, heavy with sadness as she absorbed Alec's words.

'Yes, I hope... I pray he recovers, he has so much to offer in so many ways... his job is not over yet.'

'I wish my mother and grandparents knew him as you have come to know him in such a short time.'

'Did you see the news broadcast earlier today, an announcement on crime-stoppers on the hunt for Ana, Dmitri and Boris?'

'No, I've been busy all day. It seems Aldo is hell-bent now on resolving this which is, a good thing. We cannot sit in limbo for much longer.'

Meryl's phone rang, it was Inspector Aldo urging her to hurry down to HQ. He believed they had Dmitri in custody. She was needed to identify him. They hauled in a man after an anonymous telephone call that a man fitting the crime-stoppers description was driving taxi's in Montaione. He had fake identification hence the request for confirmation that he was indeed Dmitri. Inspector Aldo promised her she would not have a face-to-face meeting with Dmitri — he would be in a line up with a few others to keep him guessing about who was identifying him and what the charges were. Meryl knew the sadistic nature of the inspector, to expect anything else was fool's hope.

Alec offered to accompany Meryl which she declined,

'I think its best you stay here, what if I'm being followed, you would be 'hot property' to the assailants still at large. Anyway, it's more important you are here with Andrei.'

'You're right, we do need to be cautious. Please call me if you need assistance.'

Ben was to be kept in the dark about this development — he would worry himself into a frenzy that might make him come rushing down to HQ at this hour.

'Good evening Ms Moorecroft,' Inspector's Aldo's voice behind her, startled her as she expected to see him sitting at his desk, 'we meet again today, things are gaining pace now — be prepared for anything. Just be warned. '

There was that travelling look again, across her body, lingering on her neck, she pulled her coat close to conceal the view he was searching for.

She did not like the sound of his comment either but decided to cooperate with whatever was needed to ensure the wheels of justice were moving forward, not backwards or who knew with the slime Aldo appeared to be, it could move sideways too!

'Where is he Inspector?'

'The viewing room is downstairs, follow me, I'll allow you some private time to decide who you believe is Dmitri. I will let you know if the one you choose is indeed the man we suspect to be him, he is using a pseudonym at the moment. Can you believe he is calling himself, Pepito? Idiot!'

Meryl looked up into the well-lit area behind the glass, it felt like she was looking into a gigantic aquarium.

Six men of varying ages looked ahead, one or two with a faint cynical smile on their faces, others looking quite unaffected — she pointed almost instantly to the man third from right in the blue jumper,

'That's him, that's unmistakably him!' The inspector who

said he was giving her private time was standing close beside her, watching her face as she selected Dmitri from the line-up.

'Thank you Ms Moorecroft, we have our man! You may go now.'

She ran out as fast as she could like a woman being chased for a crime she had committed. Alec was pacing the hospital floor like an expectant father.

'Was it him, Meryl?'

'Yes it certainly was, I have no idea what Inspector Aldo will do next, I had no direct contact with Dmitri apart from identifying him in the line-up, I would not be surprised if the inspector got some police officers as stand-ins. We will have to wait for further developments, Alec you should go off now. You've been here all day.'

'You're right Meryl, I'm emotionally exhausted today. I have to call Brad. He must be worried sick.'

'Brad?'

'Sorry Meryl, Brad is my partner in New York. With all that's been going on, I've had no time to tell you anything really about my life.'

'You should get going then, we can catch up on details tomorrow. Good night, Alec.'

'Good night, thanks again Meryl.'

Meryl sat in the visitor's room taking a walk every half hour to the window to look in on Andrei. The machine he was wired to, hummed at low volume as the pump lifted and fell like a well-oiled machine – she watched his chest heave and fall in rhythmic motion.

This felt like a waking dream, all her writing time was now consumed by hospital visits and sleepless nights. Her laptop was taken a few days ago by Inspector Aldo which put an end to all her blogging and drafting pursuits. She was filled with restless agitation in a vacuous, pensive world.

Alec's dash to call his partner made her guilty that she had not called Michael about the latest developments.

'Morrissey and Nigel', Michael Morrissey speaking.'

'Hi Michael, I see you've changed your greeting now. How are you?'

'Hello Meryl! Well thank you. Greg and I made a change late last week hoping to put a more professional edge to the business name.'

'Wow, has it been that long since our last conversation?'

'Yes, I'm afraid, we both have been pretty busy... how are things with Andrei and Inspector Aldo? Has Ben returned to London yet?'

'Michael, a lot has transpired. Ben refuses to go to London until things are resolved here which seems a long way off, I tell you. Andrei is now on life-support and Dmitri is in police custody. I had to identify him in a police line-up this evening.'

'My goodness Meryl, so much *has* happened. I'm really sorry to hear that Andrei's not doing well — this will complicate things for you and the case in general. What do you plan to do?'

'Inspector Aldo told me that I was not allowed to leave town and if there was a dire need to do so, I had to check this out with him first. My life is on hold as Andrei fights for his life ...,' she choked, cleared her throat and covered up her fragile state by saying she might be coming down with a cold.

'Take care Meryl, I wish I could be there with you, work has escalated now with so many new cases that it's impossible for me to get away anytime soon. I hope you understand, I think about you all the time. I will call you in a few days to see how Andrei is coping. Is it ok if I call Ben sometimes to keep his spirits up?'

'Thank you Michael, that would be wonderful, Ben will

appreciate hearing from you... I'm really sorry Michael....' she hung up leaving Michael feeling guilty like she always did.

Chapter 8

No legacy is as rich as honesty
Shakespeare — All's Well That Ends Well

~

A meeting with the Human Rights Commissioner for a last push to get the new workplace discrimination paper passed a little earlier was granted.

Marcia and Michael decided to take a stroll along the beach the day before the meeting to mull over all they had achieved thus far. He was also keen to hear more about Marcia's student days during the days of apartheid South Africa.

She vividly recalled the violent outbreak at the university.

'There were a series of demonstrations and boycotts of lectures leading up to the release of Nelson Mandela from prison. The university officials decided to shut the campus for a few weeks to quell the unrest. We returned home and waited for news of when we would be allowed to return to class. Six weeks later we received letters in the mail notifying us of the return to campus date. We returned with great excitement, happy to be reunited with our peers. There was an eerie quietness on the campus grounds. I attended my first lecture to a half-full class and met my mates outside the cafeteria where we chatted about what we got up to during the unexpected break. We lived at the campus residence during the academic year which meant we hailed from different parts of the country.

The stillness was soon disrupted by what sounded like gunshots and then a few raised voices coming from the direction of the administration block. Students started running and shouting out to each other to get off the grounds and take cover as riot police were approaching. More gunshot-like sounds were heard and soon the air was filled with tear-gas which was the reason for the apparent gunshots. We ran as fast as we could until we reached a steep embankment with a sheer drop to the tarmacked road below. One riot cop ran into us, I went hurtling down the thorny embankment landing in a large thorny bramble, tangled in a twisted mess. Some students' fractured arms and legs as they plunged down the embankment in a bid to escape the approaching riot cops who no doubt would have shoved us in the paddy-wagon for a stint in jail.'

'A group of male students became aggressive and lunged at a young riot cop saying, 'Look at what you've done to our women'. The young Afrikaner man, who appeared barely more than eighteen, fell to his knees crying, *'I'm sorry, jammer, jammer, so sorry, I'm just following orders. Asseblief!'* It was awful seeing him this way but the chaos around us meant that no one helped him, I have that memory plugged in my mind after all these years, he was in a situation he had no choice in, how could we condemn him?'

'We assisted each other and took a taxi into town where we realised news broadcasts around the country were announcing the disturbance at the campus after an expected peaceful return to classes. The news reported that riot police were strategically positioned on campus in the event of riotous activity. One plain-clothes officer lost his cool when a student broke a window in the administration block after he was told his student fees were in arrears. This led to the command by the officer to *attack* all students. Soon we were back home for another month until things were deemed safe to return. That was a very traumatic year both personally and academically. I swapped universities and studied at Open Universities to complete my undergrad studies. There it is, another little chapter, into my turbulent tales growing up black in an apartheid world.'

Michael walked along saying nothing, shaking his head as if replaying in his mind all that Marcia had recollected about that turbulent day at the university.

He looked at her, 'far from a 'little chapter,' Marcia. You are free from hatred or a sense of entitlement, I don't know how you do that. I had a trouble-free university life and yet I complained about everything under the sun, including the poor quality cafeteria coffee and dodged class whenever I could, I'm really ashamed to say.'

'What does hatred do but beget hatred; I don't hate the Afrikaners nor Keres Bathory, all of whom acted out of ignorance about the pain and torment they caused. The fault lies in the system that shut out the truth by letting arrogance and pride perpetuate the injustice. I prefer to channel my pain to a purpose that will, hopefully, make it better for those who become victims to such ignorance in future years. Like wars that are fuelled by power agendas and hatred, where does it get us? I have been wounded, sometimes I feel mortally wounded when I awake from a nightmare hearing a white police officer shouting, 'Get up you *kaffir!*' But I'm alive and well to tell my tale and work with someone like you to change things. How did you become so compassionate and tolerant, Michael, if you say you had a life of excess and no thought for others but yourself growing up? I had Mama Dolores who reeled me in every time I had a thought or tantrum that had a whiff of selfishness. Tell me more about Michael, the Michael before Meryl,' she implored.

He turned scarlet, 'my life is nowhere near what you have experienced, I'm not sure you want to hear any of it.'

'On the contrary my dear sir, I'm all ears, please share some of yourself, you are a closed book in many ways to me, giving your time and energy to my cause, taking nothing, giving your undivided attention to my tales of woe. Please tell me who Michael Morrissey was as he was growing up.'

'You make it difficult for me to protest any further. Here it is, brace yourself,' he laughed.

'I grew up with loving parents who would give up everything to ensure Michelle and I were educated and independent. My father shared a very close and open relationship with me as did my mother. If only you could have met her five years ago, you would understand my description of her. I had a brother, John, who died tragically in a boating accident when he was twenty-three, just two days after his birthday. He was five years older than me. I idolised him, he was a keen sportsman, he had a pick of girls — none of this went to his head — the boating accident he died in was on a scheduled race day to raise funds for the Christmas Orphanage Appeal to ensure every child in orphanages throughout the country received a gift for Christmas, not just any gift but a gift with educational value. He was involved in many such drives and often refused to accept Christmas gifts that Michelle and I fought over or complained about. He wanted nothing. He was a cool big brother. He made no secret of his lack of academic ability and worked with contentment as a motor mechanic. His death left a void that has scarred my family. He told me I should be a lawyer because I knew how to argue for what I wanted — that left its impact so I pursued a career that he suggested but instead of fighting criminal cases that come with a hefty pay cheque, I chose to work on social justice matters to keep his memory alive. Sort of my tribute to my bro, you know. Now you know what a nasty piece of work I was as a little brother.' Michael did not look up at Marcia, fearful that she had ammunition to judge him now — anxious that he had lost the allure he might have had.

She reached out, took his hand and walked on in silence.

'I believe we were meant to meet Michael, for some unknown cosmic reason, you give me hope that I can survive in this foreign land, you make me feel at home.'

Chapter 9

This cold night will turn us all to fools and madmen
Shakespeare — King Lear

~

Ana was brought in after Dmitri revealed where she was. Inspector Aldo summoned Meryl in for another line-up identification and a zooming in of the infamous hands she spoke of.

Meryl recognised Ana in an instant, that iron-rod, straight back, chin up, blank stare and the hands, the familiar hands serving hurried breakfasts and other meals, these were Ana's hardworking hands! The room spun, making her dizzy and unsteady on her feet.

Inspector Aldo spent many hours interrogating both Dmitri and Ana regarding the whereabouts of Boris Malakov. Ana and Dmitri remained tight-lipped for two days. When Inspector Aldo bargained with them on a lighter 'accomplice to the crime sentence,' Dmitri opened up, he gushed like the Niagara Falls at full swell — no censorship — a raging tsunami that was determined to destroy the shared landscape of his childhood.

Ana remained stoic.

Police searched the cottage that Boris was alleged to be staying in — two days later he was picked up at a bar, drunk and aggressive — the bar owner called police to have him removed for his unruly behaviour and insults hurled at their English clientele. Within a few hours, Inspector Aldo claimed him and had him behind bars.

The key players in Meryl's abduction and perhaps Andrei's shooter was now in custody. The three men who abducted Meryl were still at large. She would only be able to recognise their voices if she was called to identify them.

Ana's and Dmitri's refusal to accept legal representation baffled Meryl.

The trial was scheduled to begin in two weeks.

*   *   *

Alec called Meryl with the shattering news that Andrei had had another heart attack. She rushed off to the hospital that evening leaving behind a stressed and bewildered Ben.

'I don't think you should come to the hospital Ben, it might be hours before I get back.'

'Meryl, I respect your request but feel I am more in the way than any use to you during this trying time.'

'You are my oxygen in this chaos I did not plan for, please believe me when I say, you are *not* in the way, you are my advisor and dear God, I wish I had listened to you earlier... I will send you updates and call when possible.'

'Please do, I will be waiting for word.'

Inspector Aldo stood at the hospital entrance with his hands in his pocket, lost in a distant galaxy, staring up at the bright full moon.

'Inspector Aldo, good evening, how is Andrei doing?'

'Ms Moorecroft, good evening, I'm afraid it does not look good according to Professor Malakov's doctor.'

There was that horrid roving eye again! Even at a time like this, the inspector was despicable!

'I will have a word with Alec now to find out what Doctor Spartan has to say.'

'You do know that this throws a spanner in the works… regarding the commencement of the case. I'm hoping Professor Malakov pulls through to provide further evidence. I am giving it a seventy-two hour window and will make a decision thereafter.'

Meryl walked away thinking that Inspector Aldo certainly was a law unto himself, he could make decisions when the judiciary session would sit — she pondered on the power he wielded and shivered when she thought of what might occur if she chose to challenge him. Ben had warned her time and time again, to answer Inspector Aldo's questions without asking questions.

Alec sat in the waiting room, his hair dishevelled, his shirt unironed. This was a far cry from his usual immaculate, fashionable *son of Andrei dress sense*. He was a picture of a lost and grieving young man. He looked up at Meryl with pleading eyes, unable to summon a smile. She touched his shoulder in a feeble attempt to console his aching heart.

'I'm so relieved to see you.' He hugged Meryl with a familiarity that grew through their dark days of waiting for Andrei to recover.

'Are there any further updates from Doctor Spartan?'

'It's not good Meryl, the aneurysm has become dislodged but the bullet is stubbornly lodged in a precarious position. Dr Spartan says even if they do proceed, the possible outcomes are loss of speech and physical functioning and perhaps loss of mental capacity too…

what hope is that huh — ?' His voice broke off. Meryl held both his hands trying to calm both their growing fears.

'You will have to take a decision on that Alec... but at least he's alive, is that not worth fighting for?'

'He cannot be left mentally incapacitated... a man of his intellect and academic standing... it would be sinful to allow that... or to keep him alive in this condition... I know he would want me to ensure he was not — a living vegetable... I cannot bear it any longer ...'

They sat lost in their own reveries both carrying the increasing weight of this moment.

*　　*　　*

Michael called at 9 pm. Meryl stepped outside into the chilly night air to take the call. He was excited and happy to announce to Meryl without picking up on her subdued tone:

'Meryl! I have some great news! The Ntuli case has been considered by the Human Rights Commission as worthy to refresh workplace harassment, not just in schools but in all workplace arenas! I'm stoked as is Marcia who is leaving to South Africa in a few weeks.'

A long silence on Meryl's end stifled Michael's exuberance.

'Is everything okay Meryl?'

'I'm so happy for you Michael. No, sadly, Andrei has deteriorated and Alec faces a very difficult decision and there are legal matters to contend with too, regarding whether it is his call to decide the next step for Andrei.'

Hearing himself being addressed twice formally as 'Michael', not 'Mike' or the endearing 'Mikey' made him realise that he should have asked after Andrei before plunging headlong into his victory.

'I am so sorry to hear this Meryl. I could check on the law requirements there given Alec's circumstances… if that's ok with you… I'm so sorry my timing is poor and it was insensitive of me to expect you to share in my joy, right now. I could call you back later…'

'No Michael, you have every right to be happy with the outcome on this case, this is my cross to bear. It will be good for your business profile too. This is great news. I'll call you when I get back to the hotel.'

*   *   *

Ben's growing concern that Meryl might be hooked too deeply in the barbed justice wrangle on the Malakov case made him lapse into long silences as Meryl chatted on beyond midnight. He called a neighbour of many years to keep an eye on his property and the lawn-mowing service to tidy up his front garden. He knew the stay in Florence was going to be longer than he envisaged. His adept organisational skills were of no use to Meryl now who floated through the days, waiting to be given word on what was expected of her.

They finally settled on giving themselves two weeks before they decided when they would return to London. Meryl was acutely aware that she was under instruction not to leave Florence.

Chapter 10

*Not all the water in the rude rough sea can wash the
balm from an anointed king.*
Shakespeare — Richard II

~

Inspector Aldo scheduled a meeting with Meryl and Alec.
Meryl asked if Ben could be invited to the meeting. Inspector
Aldo denied this request saying it was not necessary at this stage
to involve Ben. Meryl squirmed at the irony of the inspector's
comment, he had made it quite clear on many occasions that
he was suspicious of Ben's involvement in the shooting.

Alec was asked to shed light on his family circumstances.
Inspector Aldo asked Meryl to leave the room, Alec, quite out
of character, demanded that Meryl be present. The inspector
for once had to concede if he hoped to get any information
from Alec.

'My father was a hands-on father despite his many academic
commitments — he turned up to school events, sporting events
as a parent would.'

'What about your mother?'

'She was always busy in her father's business. She was never
home. Ana and her mother ran our home, preparing meals,

cleaning the house and doing our laundry. Dmitri's father was the family driver who took us, that is Boris and I to school and school events, always waiting in the car until we were finished.'

'I see, hence your closeness to your father. Interesting that Ana and Dmitri were part of your childhood years. What can you tell me about your brother Boris growing up?'

'Boris was always angry, even as a child. He was often involved in fights with school-mates and the neighbourhood children. He was very close to our grandfather, our mother's father. He had a close friendship with Dmitri who always did his bidding, helping him out of fights with other kids and protecting him from getting into trouble with our father.'

'How is it that Ana and Dmitri ended up working for your father in Florence? Why did they leave Russia?'

'Due to my parents' marital strife and my mother's unstinting allegiance to my grandfather, she left the house and moved back to her childhood home. Boris was already living with our grandfather from the age of five.'

He shook his head as the memories flooded back.

'I stayed at the house with my father for a few months until he moved to New York. During this period Ana's mother and Dmitri's father passed away and the family home was shut.'

His leg twitched with agitation as the pain of this terrible time in his young life resurfaced. He paused and continued,

'Andrei being the man he is, could not desert Ana and Dmitri who really grew up around him even though they also worked some hours for my grandfather. He later arranged to have them work for him in Florence. Ana was well taken care of. When Andrei was out of town she did not have to seek work. My father was very generous to Dmitri too, allowing him to earn whatever he wanted when he was not driving Andrei around in Florence.'
His voice trailed off, heavy with emotion as he concluded,

'It has become clear that they did not appreciate what he did for them and they appear to have given their allegiance to Boris.'

'Thank you for that, we are yet to be informed regarding their involvement in Andrei's shooting and of course Ms Moorecroft's abduction. We are going on suppositions regarding your brother's involvement. I will ask you a few more questions soon, I will now turn to Ms Moorecroft. What more can you shed on the character of Professor Malakov although, as we know, you knew him briefly?'

'Do not speak of Andrei in the past tense, we, Alec and I have hope that… Andrei will pull through.'

'No malicious intent, I assure you, please continue.'

'Yes, I have known Andrei for all of two months during which time I came to appreciate his academic contributions and love of Shakespeare and his research and writing of a definitive biography on Shakespeare. We went to dinners and the opera until he invited me to enjoy the quiet and space to pursue my writing aims.'

'So you were in a romantic relationship, I take it?'

'No sir, a very close bond of friendship based on mutual respect is how I would define my relationship with Andrei. I have said this to you several times!'

'I see, so no romantic feelings, no… intimacy… you say,' he shot a raised eyebrow-look in Alec's direction and continued, 'you understand I have to ask these questions because you might know more than you think you do, should you have shared intimate moments… conversations as lovers, yes?' His roving eyes travelled in their customary sleazy way, resting this time on Meryl's lips.

'We certainly had intimate conversations regarding his marriage to Mariya and his difficulty in attaining his divorce, hence his departure to Russia while I was in Viareggio. We are and were not lovers, I reiterate once again, Inspector Aldo. I would like you to record that in your notes please.'

It took every ounce of restraint for Meryl to say this in respect of her friendship with Andrei. How dare the Inspector suggest they were in some love tryst!

'Aha! So a closeness existed... I could ask Alec to leave the room if it makes you uncomfortable to talk about your relationship, albeit fleeting with Professor Malakov?'

This was more than Meryl could bear, she sucked in her breath – this malicious man was every sense a dog with a bone or a dog in heat.

'I have made it quite clear and will do so again and again, my relationship with Professor Malakov is platonic, Alec does not have to leave the room, we are both adults and what I have said will not change if he is out of earshot, in this life or the next, if I should be lucky to have another Inspector Aldo!' Her hands trembled and her voice quivered as she fought to rein in her emotions.

'Ok! I get that Ms Moorecroft! Recount a bit about your first meeting, in Bath I recall.'

He continued to harangue her on the same details. She was aware that his aim was to discredit her to Alec, to prove she was some conniving hussy!

'I was sitting at the table in the teashop when Andrei approached me to borrow a chair. We met on the bus later and chatted a bit more. He was with a group of nine travellers some of whom I met again at dinner and the opera in London.' She rushed through this recount on fast rewind.

'You shared contact details on the bus I take it?'

'Yes, you recorded all of this in our last meeting, inspector. Why am I going over this again?'

'You will be asked the same questions again during the trial

Ms Moorecroft so think of this as your rehearsal. Did you find Professor Malakov aggressive at all?'

Meryl drew a deep breath and continued;

'I did hear him speak a little harshly on the telephone a few times to someone, he spoke in Russian. Both times he said it was his elder son who was 'difficult' at times. He was never aggressive to me nor did I notice him being aggressive to his staff.'

'Can you remember specifically the times you heard him speak with anger on the telephone? Could you provide a date for each of these occasions?'

'The first time would have to be when we were on our way to the opera in London to see *The Phantom of the Opera*. He received a call on the way to the theatre when he spoke with a harsh tone in Russian to the person on the other end. He was a little agitated but told me it was nothing to be concerned about. He was composed at dinner with a few of his friends, part of the group I met in Bath. In the middle of the first act he excused himself to take another call. He was gone for a long time and returned at the beginning of Act 2. He apologised but appeared unsettled for the second time that evening. That occurred on 11th November. The next time I perceived his agitation was at the cottage in Viareggio, he was talking quite loudly on the telephone in his study obviously in argument with the caller. Soon after that he told me he had to go to Russia for a few days to sort out matters with Mariya. This was two weeks after the time at the opera, I'm afraid I cannot recall the date specifically of the second display of tension.' Meryl was exhausted from this mental interrogation.

'Was there anything else out of character that you noticed — I know you did not know him long enough — you are a writer, hence a great observer and scholar of human behaviour, did you notice anything else about him that might have been of some concern to you?'

Meryl looked across at Alec who was staring blankly at the floor.

'I'm not sure what to make of this, but, Andrei was not in Florence to pick me up from the airport as promised. A cab driver transported me to the apartment and the housekeeper indicated that Andrei was in Pelago for the day attending to family matters. I was a little miffed at first that he neglected to let me know that his plans had changed.'

'The cab driver, was he Dmitri? Pelago? Mmmmm... Alec do you know who your father might have seen in Pelago?'

'Not really sure inspector, he did have an old friend who lived there at one time. Only he will be able to shed light on that;' Alec said.

Meryl looked the inspector straight in the eye, 'the cab driver was not Dmitri, and I assume he drove Andrei to Pelago, but, I cannot confirm that, you will have to ask him that question.'

'I suppose it will come to light at some point. You have a lot to deal with now young man, you have to decide what care... if any... your father will receive now. Keep me informed, and should anything come to mind, do not dismiss it as trivial, call me, we need everything we can find with Professor Malakov incapacitated as he is.'

'Inspector,' Meryl said, 'the night I was taken from the cottage in Viareggio, I heard one voice, a male voice saying they were looking for the manuscript for *Time* magazine.

'Alec, would you be able to add some clarity to this?'

'I was not too involved in my father's professional life, however, I'm aware he was writing an article of some sort on my grandfather's business in Moscow.'

'Interesting... that sounds like content, important content

for our next meeting. Hold that thought Alec. I bid you both a very good night and thank you for your cooperation.'

The sickening glint in his eye was unmistakable.

Meryl looked at Alec as Inspector Aldo left the room.

'I am really over this badgering by the inspector, he is constantly prying for personal details that are unnecessary to the case. It seems he is trying to dig up something that is not there to cause a rift between us. Do you feel the same way Alec?'

'I think he is peeved that you have him somewhat sussed out. The personal attacks are aggravating but we cannot get on the wrong side of this man, there is an uncanny, almost insane vibe that I pick up,'

'Yes, he's an odd man, I am of the same opinion and need to keep my temper in check around him.'

Chapter 11

Sound trumpets! Let our bloody colours wave! —
(Shakespeare — Henry VI Part III)

~

M onths of hard work was finally recognised. This was a
landmark moment that workplace harassment was to
be addressed within shorter time-frames with full external,
neutral support for the victim. Privileged institutions could
no longer sweep dirt under the rug, it was mandatory now that
even the slightest whiff of harassment had to be reported to the
Human Rights Commission who would then bring in external
parties to objectively assess the situation.

Marcia sat down in Michael's office, radiating relief,

'Thank you so much Michael, I could not be happier, what an
achievement! This stretch we have been on together with the five
years of pain I went through has not been in vain! That others
will be 'taken care of' with the full support of the Human Rights
Commission is all I need to know. Without your guidance and
support I would have been a snivelling mess going from one seda-
tive to another. 'Thank you' sounds empty and, insubstantial
now in the wake of all you sacrificed to make this possible.'

Michael sat listening to Marcia canonise him for something
he loved doing, the way she saw him was not how he viewed

himself. He looked up at her, his ears burned, his face was scarlet as he shook his head. 'You make me seem saintly when I know I'm not. To see you transformed to this moment from the nervous woman standing in the rain outside my office is the only thanks I need. You gave me the opportunity to moot for changed law, this is huge in my professional world and you wanted nothing. All I can say is that I'm grateful that you came along when you did. You have given me a few life lessons on tolerance and unwavering inner strength.'

He walked across to Marcia and hugged her like an old friend, not a lover, not a besotted boy but a friend he respected and admired for her selflessness. He knew his job was not over, the media would pursue him and he had a duty to protect Marcia from their harsh, insensitive glare.

'Do you have leave available Michael? Can you get away for two to three weeks? I want to show you the South Africa I grew up in, I want you to come with me.'

He was speechless at first. It was almost as if she had read his mind.

'Wow! Yes, Marcia I can leave in two weeks, Greg is back from his vacation, he will gladly cover for me. The Human Rights Commission has everything in place and I will be a telephone call away although I doubt I will be needed for at least six weeks.'

'Great! Can you leave, on Tuesday the 18th? I can get us on that flight to Johannesburg. I have been keeping a close eye on the flights out and seats are available on the 18th.'

Michael called Greg who was pleased that he was finally taking a break. They would work through what needed to be 'looked after' on Michael's end while he was away.

Marcia looked up at Michael, 'Will you tell Meryl about your trip soon?'

'I will, perhaps in a day or two, Andrei has had a few setbacks. The trial is scheduled to begin sometime soon — she has a lot happening now, but yes, I will tell her, later perhaps.'

Marcia knew that this trip meant a lot to Michael — it was to be her demonstration of her gratitude to him for making her whole again, making her believe in herself again.

*   *   *

Meryl was over the moon that Michael was taking a much-needed break. She offered her congratulations on the victory. She filled him in on her meeting with Inspector Aldo but could not bring herself to tell him that the speculating inspector insinuated on several occasions that she was in a love affair with Andrei. Michael cautioned her that the inspector was deceptive enough to attempt to mislead her with his fleeting moments of civility.

Ben was sitting up in bed with a mug of cocoa when Meryl looked in on him.

'I'm concerned that those three scoundrels that were involved in kidnapping you, have not been found. Why does it appear that the inspector is dragging his heels on this? Something tells me there's far more to this horrible man!'

'I agree, I have taken your advice to 'answer questions without asking questions,' she laughed. 'My wrists are still little sore from those days of being bound together.' She rubbed her wrists as she spoke, 'Its late now, we can take care of it in the morning.'

Ben pulled out his ever-ready jar of soothing arnica balm and gently rubbed it into her aching wrists.

Meryl had a fitful night — her world became more complicated with each passing day.

*   *   *

Grandpa Joshua's funeral floated into her dream. She was thirteen years old. Grandma Beth had passed away two years earlier.

The smell of white roses and incense burning in the heat of that summer day made her feel sick, she was sweaty and tired and the speeches seemed to come from voices that echoed from another realm — she needed air — the chapel was crowded with a sea of heads, bald heads, most them, that floated around when she looked up. Nobody was there to console her — Uncle Ben was at a conference in Greece — he was arriving later the next day.

She felt herself being dragged, floating heads and soft voices in a fog until soon all was dark.

A cold, wet cloth across her face brought her gasping into a sitting position, Aunty Alice, Grandpa Josh's youngest sister was holding onto to her.

'You ok Merrie? You fainted in the chapel. Did you have breakfast? We are going to sit here for a while in the cool air.'

'No Aunty Alice, I didn't have breakfast, I woke up feeling queasy this morning. Thank you for bringing me outside, I hope I was not too heavy to carry out.'

'Heavy? Nonsense! You're as light as a feather young lady. Let's sit here quietly for a bit now. Here, have a sip of water.'

She whispered a faint, 'thank you,' and leaned on Alice until Grandpa Joshua's coffin was brought out to the hearse for the drive to the crematorium.

*   *   *

Meryl got out of bed and turned on the television, her dream had left her exhausted and edgy. She flicked through channels until she found a repeat of a news broadcast that announced grave concerns for the life of Professor Andrei Malakov.

An inside report from Florence's cardiac unit has confirmed today that Professor Andrei Malakov has had a further setback in his recovery. No one was available to make comment at Florence Hospital on whether the trial was to proceed as scheduled.

Professor Malakov has made valuable contributions in literature here in Florence and has been reported to be working on research into William Shakespeare's life revealing aspects never before researched nor found. We hope to bring you more later tomorrow on Professor Malakov's condition.

Meryl was not happy that there seemed to be an inside source feeding information to the media. She contemplated telling Inspector Aldo that there was a potential threat to the case and thought better of it.

Inspector Aldo's political and media associations made her suspicious that he might be the 'inside source.' She would sound her thoughts with Alec in the morning.

Meryl had a voicemail message to call Alec urgently.

Andrei's lawyer from Pelago wanted to see them urgently. He was scheduled to arrive in town on Wednesday morning and wanted to meet around 3 pm that afternoon at the hospital.

Chapter 12

Meantime we shall express our darker purpose
— Give me the map there.
Shakespeare — King Lear

~

Meryl had another troubled night's sleep after hearing that Andrei's lawyer, Gildo Mondo wanted to see her too. She was wound up and worried that *she* was being called in to meet with him — she was a newcomer in Andrei's life, what could he possibly want with her? She remembered that Andrei was in Pelago when she arrived in Florence. Ana indicated that he was attending to family matters there.

Andrei did not offer any explanations for his sudden trip to Pelago. The puzzle was about to unfold.

Ben had become a silent observer ever since Meryl's last meeting with Inspector Aldo. He listened to all Meryl's concerns and offered advice only when he thought it would serve to keep her safe with whatever she was dealing with.

'Meryl, the lawyer wanting to see you might be something Andrei had stipulated he do, it was clearly apparent that Andrei was smitten with you from my one and only encounter with him on the evening of the opera you both attended. I suspect this is why he took action after a period of dormancy to speed up the divorce. Take it in a positive light, he trusted you, rightfully so, he knew you sooner than you thought possible. Go with no expectations and listen but please, dear Meryl, I have to say this, please do not say anything, just listen and talk to Alec after the meeting. These legal eagles worry me sometimes, one never knows what their agenda might be. Michael is an exception, of course,' he smiled and looked up at Meryl waiting for her response.

'Yes Ben, I will listen and try not to complicate things for myself. I'm really saddened that I cannot go ahead with my blog entries under instruction from Inspector Aldo. I've started handwriting in journals now and pray that the inspector does not confiscate those too. I need my laptop — I've been forbidden to post anything online.'

'It's for the best Meryl, you do not want to incriminate yourself in any way, even if it's to satisfy the creative urge in you.'

'I know, I know, I did not plan for this Ben, fate cast its hand in my direction — I blame Shakespeare for this,' she laughed.

'Well, it's good to hear you laugh my dear, I've missed that recently.'

*   *   *

Gildo Mondo, a man who appeared to be in his early sixties, sat in the hospital waiting room chatting to Alec when Meryl arrived. He was a short, stout, stooped man with a thick greying moustache that framed his rather bulbous lips, his bushy eyebrows sat in a perpetual frown which concealed a clear view of his eyes. Meryl always judged people at a first encounter on their eyes, the size, shape and moods they reflected. Gildo Mondo made Meryl feel uncomfortable as he stood up with an extended hand to greet her, barely looking at her. Both his rather soft hands encased her hand putting her at ease in this humble gesture. Perhaps he was not someone to distrust, or be fearful of, just yet.

'Good afternoon, Ms Moorecroft, good to finally meet you.' The first words out of the bulbous lipped cavity made Meryl uneasy again.

'Meryl, please. 'Finally meet' …?' Meryl stopped, wondering what Mondo knew about her.

'All good I assure you Ms Meryl, please let's sit together and go through what I have to say.'

Alec motioned to the doctor's office for privacy away from prying eyes in the waiting room.

Gildo Mondo continued regarding how sorry he was that Andrei was not recovering as all had hoped, he raised concerns on the news broadcast that presented dire claims on Andrei's health, hence his premature visit. Alec enquired why his visit was 'premature.'

I was appointed to draw up or rather to rewrite your father's last will and testament which he has signed. The instruction was that should he pass on or was mentally and physically incapacitated, both you and Meryl Moorecroft were to be notified that he nominated you as executors of his estate. You can now understand why after hearing that news broadcast I decided to see you both.' Gildo Mondo surveyed Meryl as he spoke, watching like an eagle, ready to pounce on anything — her body language — her questions — her comments.

Meryl remained silent as Ben had cautioned and looked at Alec to say the first word.

'This is surreal, being named the executor of my father's estate — I have never given this a thought, never considered this at all and now, this — this moment now… does not seem real.' Alec's uncertainty left Meryl in an even more vulnerable position under the watchful eye of Gildo Mondo.

'What do you have to say Ms Meryl?' Gildo Mondo asked.

'I'm surprised that I've been given co-executorship of Andrei's estate, so please forgive me as I am still trying to process this... Andrei is still alive, is this not premature on your part... sir?'

'I can understand your shock, I questioned Andrei on this point myself, to ensure he was absolutely clear about this decision as I am aware you two were in the process of getting to know each other.' Mondo said this with slow, deliberate emphasis while studying Meryl's reactions.

Alec moved closer to Meryl. Her face was lined with worry as she thought, 'dear god, Mondo thinks I am a money grabbing harlot!'

Alec, with the gentle nature of his father, reached out for Meryl's hand and held onto it in quiet assurance that he appreciated her being there. He then said in whispered tones,

'My father is very much alive Mr Mondo, thank you for rushing over with this information but it is not something, Meryl and I need concern ourselves with at this point. My father's restoration to mental and physical wellbeing is our priority.'

'I assure you, I appreciate this and apologise if I appear insensitive. Inspector Aldo called me regarding the case and suggested I speed things up as time was running out.'

'Running out, for what?' Alec asked with raised concern, 'what does he know about my father's decision to name us as executors of his estate?'

'I think he meant the hearing — hence he wanted all parties to be in the know as it were.' Mondo said this with no eye contact with either Meryl or Alec. Mondo stood up quite suddenly saying he would be in contact again soon and hurried off without the first formality of a handshake.

Alec was crestfallen — 'All parties,' he said, 'including Inspector Aldo?'

'Look, we have to focus on what's important now, firstly getting Andrei well with our positive energy and secondly be prepared for the perpetrators to be brought to justice.'

'Yes Meryl, Andrei did not deserve this, from Boris or anyone else.'

'What was the issue with the hunt for the *Time* magazine manuscript Andrei was working on?' Meryl asked.

'That is a long and complicated story that I am not too clued up on although I know Andrei was not happy with child labour exploitation and my grandfather's shoe industry was under scrutiny for this.'

'Goodness, this is larger and deeper than I thought — it's not just about Andrei's divorce as I had imagined.'

'I suppose we both shall learn a lot more during the trial, I feel sick thinking about it Meryl. I am so sorry too that you got innocently enmeshed in this.'

'No Alec, I did go into my friendship with Andrei based on admiration and as a willing adult — please don't worry on my account, you have a lot to deal with. I will be here until Andrei and you can find a way forward in your lives.'

'I can see why Andrei was drawn to you — it's a lot to bear with Boris' involvement in all of this too. Who knows what will happen to him now? Andrei will wish no harm upon him which worries me that he might do this again.'

'Be guided by your conscience and faith in all things Alec, that's the only way now.'

Meryl felt odd dishing out such advice that she herself needed to abide by.

*   *   *

Meryl and Ben sat solemnly at dinner.

'Meryl, are you going to be able to handle the media scrutiny once this has leaked to them, as things like this do?'

'I will have to brace myself for a lot more with the imminent trial and the ruthless questions that will be asked about my 'association' with the 'roving professor,' more so than ever if it leaks out that I am named as co-executor of Andrei's estate. Inspector Aldo has mentioned that Andrei was on their radar for his frequent jaunts across the US, Europe and England and the so called 'wild' parties at the villa in Viareggio — my concern is that there is much more that might emerge in the trial — I need to fortify myself for what might emerge rather than the media tearing my reputation to shreds. And I have you — I will overcome whatever comes with you holding my hand as always.'

Ben looked up — these past weeks had exhausted him, he had grown thinner and paler. He did not have the heart to tell her that he was feeling the weight of all that was going on in her world and the discomfit of living without the old and familiar in London.

Chapter 13

Make room, and let him stand before our face
Shakespeare — The Merchant of Venice

~

D ay one of the trial was in session.
It was a cloudy day with light rain in Florence. Media
hype regarding Andrei's case brought crowds of people to the
courthouse. Andrei, reclusive for most of his life, was known to
some local residents for his friendly smile and cursory greeting
when they encountered him on rare occasions. He had spent
almost two decades in and out of Florence, staying at the villa
in Viareggio for periods of yearned solitude and as Inspector
Aldo revealed, as host to a few 'wild parties.' Meryl hoped to ask
Andrei, when he recovered from his injuries, what the inspector
meant by this. This did not fit the perception she had of Andrei.

Ben, Meryl, Alec and Brad, Alec's partner, who had arrived
the day before, sat huddled in one row in the courtroom.

Dmitri was the first to be called to the stand.

'State your full name,' the prosecutor said.

'Dmitri Repin.'

'What is the nature of your work in Florence?'

'I am a taxi driver sir.'

'Which company do you work for?'

'I run my own business as a taxi driver.'

'What is your association with Professor Andrei Malakov?'

'I work as a chauffeur for him whenever he is in Florence.'

'How long have you known Professor Malakov?'

'A long time, not sure how long.'

'You have to be more specific Mr Repin.'

'Maybe about nineteen or twenty years.'

'A long time, time enough for you to know Professor Malakov very well.'

Dmitri remained silent.

'Is that right Mr Repin?' urged the prosecutor

'I suppose.'

'What made you come to Florence from Russia to work as a taxi driver, Mr Repin?'

'Professor Malakov, he arranged to bring me to Florence.'

'Oh, so you have a long-standing relationship with Andrei Malakov. You then should have a great allegiance to him, am I right?'

Meryl sat close to Ben listening to Dmitri answering questions with limited depth — this was the first time she heard him speak as many words — he came across as the strong, silent type, simmering beneath a placid exterior, this was how she thought he presented when she first met him at the villa.

The prosecutor, an impish looking man, paced the floor, his right hand on his chin, his deep frown, veiled the hardness of his eyes. The light rain of the morning had passed, a short-lived storm — then brief sunshine until heavy clouds were set to remain overhead.

He continued his questioning.

'Explain to the court with all the details you can remember on how and why Professor Malakov brought you to Florence.'

'Like I said, to be his chauffeur, he liked me in Russia and that made him offer me work here.'

'Where did you meet in Russia, Mr Repin? Let's not make this any more difficult.'

The judge, a poker-faced, pixie-eared man who had an odd way of holding his head in a peculiar partial tilt to the left, looked up from his paperwork,

'I urge that the questions are direct, without any insinuations,' he ordered.

'I beg the court's pardon, your Honour. Continue Mr Repin, where did you get to know the professor in Russia?'

'I worked for Aleksandra Moisey, Professor Malakov's father-in-law, in his shoe factory – that is where I met Mr Andrei.'

'Ah, now the pattern is forming,' said the prosecutor, rubbing his chin with his right hand. How long did you work in the factory before the professor approached you to come to Florence?'

'A long time, from about the age of thirteen.'

'How old were you when you arrived in Florence?'

'I was twenty-one, an adult.'

'How long have you been working for Professor Malakov? Please be specific?'

'Twenty years, on and off as he is not always in Florence.'

'What is your association with Ana Kuznetsov?'

'No association sir.'

'Let me rephrase this, how long have you known Ana?'

'She worked for Mr Malakov's mother-in-law, at least her mother did.'

'Did you both come to Florence to work for the professor at the same time?'

'No sir, Ana was already here some eighteen months before I got here.'

'Would you say you both had a good working relationship?'

'Well, we were not close, we just worked for Mr Andrei.'

'What was your relationship with Professor Malakov like?'

After a long silence, the prosecutor paced the floor in meditative stance, his eyes completely covered by his drooping frown.

'We had a good relationship.'

'Can you describe what he was like in your working relationship?'

'He was a kind man who did not interfere with what I did when he was away from Florence.'

'Did he 'interfere' when he was here then?'

Dmitri had no legal representation by choice, he answered the prosecutor's questions with no sign of stress nor agitation, he continued in his bland manner,

'No, no, I won't say that, but I had to be around to drive wherever he wanted to go, he said he spent so much time travelling that he preferred to be driven around when he got home. He called Florence 'home."

'That will be all for now, Mr Repin,' the prosecutor said as he looked up at the judge, 'shall we stop for half an hour before we resume with our next witness, your Honour?'

The judge agreed that a recess was in order.

*   *   *

The rain had dried up, a cool breeze wafted into the courtroom as everyone cleared out for a short break.

Meryl, Ben and Alec sat together on the bench outside when Ben broke in to their thoughts,

'Repin seems a nice enough person, do you think he had anything to do with Meryl's kidnapping and Andrei being shot, Alec?'

'He's a dark horse is what I remember of him on the very few occasions I visited my father here in Florence. He was not one to say much, I don't really know him to be honest.'

'That's pretty much my perception of Dmitri too, I don't think he took my presence too kindly at Viareggio. Andrei indicated both he and Ana were trusted staff.' Meryl frowned more these days which claimed her radiant smile that once drew people to her.

'I'll hail a cab and head back to the hotel Meryl and wait to hear what the rest of the questioning was like. If you want me to stay back, I will,' said Ben.

'You should go back Ben, I will stop at the hospital and then head back to you. I will more than likely keep you up tonight as usual.'

'I have some mail to catch up on and a few telephone calls to make and yes a rest, more like a nap, thereafter sounds precisely what the doctor would order today,' Ben laughed.

Brad said he would go back to the apartment too as he had some matters to attend to.

Meryl and Alec waved Ben and Brad off and strolled around the courtyard of the courthouse.

'You are so lucky Meryl to have Ben who is stoically behind you, it's a rarity in family relationships; I tell you. I saw so much dissension with my mother's family. Andrei grew up, in a wonderful loyal family which did not exist in his marriage to my mother. I think that is what might have drawn you both together, what do you think?'

'One could say the same with Brad dropping everything to be here to support you through the trial Alec. He seems to be a kind, caring person. Who knows what attracts people to each other? Andrei's ability to put me at ease and his knowledge of the literary world made for marvellous hours of conversations just as I have with Ben. You know your father very well or

have a discerning appreciation of the make-up of individuals.'
She hooked her arm through his as they headed back into the
courtroom.

Ana Kuznetsov was called to testify on the part she played
in the events that led to Andrei being shot.

Meryl looked at Ana as she walked up to the stand, her back
was straight and taut, her chin slightly elevated and her countenance that of one who was only physically present as she floated
to the front of the courtroom with a supernatural aura. Meryl
remembered that fateful, stormy night at the villa in Viareggio,
Ana's wild hair and cold attitude the night before her world
changed forever. She shivered as she recalled the meals served
to her when she was locked away from light and love behind a
large, impenetrable steel door.

What Ana was about to reveal left all, including Gildo
Mondo, in a state of confused disbelief.

Chapter 14

*My resolutions placed, and I have nothing of woman
in me; now from head to foot I am marble*
Shakespeare — *Anthony and Cleopatra*

~

'I am Ana Kuznetsov, housekeeper to Professor Malakov, I
have been working for him for twenty years.'

The prosecutor walked in Ana's direction tapping his chin
with his forefinger as he approached her. He looked up from
beneath his flourishing frown looking right through Ana, he
proceeded,

'Would that be before or after Signor Repin began working
for Professor Malakov?'

'I started working a year before Signor Repin?'

'Can you explain how you knew the professor before you
began working for him, here in Florence?'

'My mother worked for Professor Malakov's mother-in-law
as housekeeper and my father was one of the drivers appointed
to the family.'

'How did it come about that you ended up in Professor Malakov's employ?'

'Miss Mariya's father, Aleksandra Moisey, Professor

Malakov's father-in law had a shoe factory and all the children of his staff were expected to work at the factory after school, once we turned thirteen we had to work there full time... Professor Malakov was not happy with this, he believed children had to have a childhood.'

'How do you know the professor was not happy with this?'

'We, the children, used to hear the arguments between Miss Mariya and the professor about her father's expectations placed on young children who should be educated first and then allowed to make their choices.'

'Go on, when did the professor move to Florence?'

'He had the villa for many years, he moved in and out of Russia over the years as you know, sir, spending more time out of Russia as his marriage was not good when he started being unhappy about the treatment of staff's children. Many, many arguments were overheard.'

'Were you unhappy working in the shoe factory?'

'It was a job, my parents earned very little as housekeeper and driver and what hours I put in, helped as we were given grocery packs.'

'Grocery packs? No payment in cash?'

The judge's annoyance with the prosecutor's line of questioning was evident when he told him to keep to the gist of what was needed, Ana's form of payment was irrelevant to the case on hand.

'I withdraw that question, Ms Kuznetsov. Please provide the details of how you were enlisted to work for Professor Malakov?'

'Professor Malakov moved with his son, Alec, to Florence, he needed to have someone to oversee the boy who was living with him so he offered me the position of nanny and housekeeper.'

'Ah... what about his son Boris, did he come to Florence too?'

Ana was silent this time, she cleared her throat and looked

directly at Inspector Aldo in the public gallery. His fiery look was menacing enough to make Ana hurriedly look away.

'No Mr Boris did not come, he was very close to his grandfather and chose to remain in Russia with his mother.'

'So Boris and his father are known to be, shall I say, on 'not so friendly terms', agreed Ms Kuznetsov?'

Another long pause.

'I suppose, he spent more time at his grandparents' home.'

'How long did you look after Alec in Florence?'

'Just to settle him in for two months then he was sent to boarding school so I did not see much of him unless Professor Malakov was around in the school holidays.'

'What do you do when the professor is out of town, as he is most of the time, as a roving professor?'

'Professor Malakov sent me for sewing classes so I do tailoring work for women as a business from the apartment in the city.'

'How often did the Professor come to Florence?'

'Once in three months for short periods of time and maybe longer in the summer.'

'Would his son Alec join him in the summer when he was in Florence?'

'Not always, they spent more time in New York together.'

'Are you close to Professor Malakov?'

'I appreciate what he has done for me as I might not have had my freedom as I do here if I was still working in the shoe factory.'

'Is it fair to say that you do not really know Alec and Boris very well?'

Ana's faint, 'yes' left the prosecutor pensive and suspicious, his eyebrows lay in a low unbalanced frown, the left brow arched while the right brow became straight as he paced the floor.

'Was that a 'yes', Ms Kuznetsov?'

Ana nodded her.

'I require a verbal response please, Ms Kuznetsov?'

'I did not know Alec very well but Boris maybe a bit better.'

'How did that come about?'

'My father took Boris to school as the family driver and often I was in the car on my way to the factory.'

'Is it a friendship that you share with Boris then?'

'I suppose it is.'

'Where are your parents now Ms Kuznetsov?'

'My parents passed away many years ago.'

'Do you have other family in Russia?'

'A cousin who works for Ms Mariya.'

'Male or female cousin?'

'Male?'

'What work does he do for Ms Mariya?'

'Takes care of her property, I think.'

'Am I to assume you do not keep in touch with your cousin Ms Kuznetsov?'

'I do but not very often.'

'Did you know Boris was in Florence when Ms Moorecroft was kidnapped?'

Meryl studied Ana's facial expressions and body language, she felt tense, expecting to hear her confirm that she was indeed the woman who brought Meryl her meals when she was locked away behind the steel door.

'Yes I knew he was in Florence because he rang me to say he was coming?'

'Is this why you left Ms Meryl at the villa in Viareggio to return to the city?'

'Boris never came to Viareggio whenever he was in Italy, he always stayed in rented apartments or with friends.'

'You have not answered my question, Ms Kutznetsov.'

'No sir, I had some work to do in Florence, some sewing work I promised that is all.'

'I see, so Boris Malakov does have friends here, yes... interesting.'

Meryl was aware that Ana was losing her cool as the prosecutor fired questions at her. Her breaking point appeared close, she swayed back and forth in her seat like an agitated spectator of her own game, hell-bent on not giving the prosecutor the victory.

'Ms Kuznetsov, I do believe you are not telling us everything about Boris Malakov. If he called you to tell you he was going to be in Florence, you surely must have known the reason for his visit.'

'I don't question what he does, he lets me know he is coming to arrange for his cooking and cleaning.'

'Cooking and cleaning? Did he stay with you then?'

'No, he used to send someone to pick up food from me.'

'You both have a close bond and you need to remember that you are in a court of law, under oath; withholding information is detrimental to the process and yourself.'

The judge raised his head like Rip Van Winkle after his eternal slumber pronouncing every syllable in a hiss,

'Ms Kuznetsov, it is imperative that you do not withhold any information with regards to Boris Malakov.'

Ana blurted out, 'Boris Malakov is my younger half-brother, we have the same father.'

The hush over the courtroom amplified the sound of light rain falling on the courtroom roof that afternoon.

'This session will resume on Monday morning at 10 am,' the judge announced.

Hurried, tapping of heels on the wooden floorboards broke

the silence as people rushed out with diverted eyes, fearing being drawn into a conversation on the bomb Ana had just dropped.

*   *   *

They departed, each hailed a taxi with the same solemness yielded by Ana's final comment.

As his taxi approached, Alec looked at Meryl, 'I'll call you in the morning.'

'Take care Alec,' she called out without glancing in his direction, knowing the pain he must be in and not knowing what other truths would emerge in their conversation the next day.

Meryl stared out the window on the drive to the hotel, a million miles away in a cloud of confusion.

She called Ben, 'I will come over to see you soon, much has happened, things become more complicated by the moment, I cannot imagine what else will be revealed or what really is true in all of this. I am close to packing up and leaving if it was up to me!' She knew she was blabbering on in an incomprehensible stringing of words. She had to process it all first.

'I'll see you in an hour.' She lay staring at the ceiling, mentally and emotionally drained.

Chapter 15

...a perilous voyage to an unknown land...
Shakespeare — Twelfth Night

~

Marcia was packed and waiting at Michael's door bright and early for their flight to Johannesburg. He met her as the taxi arrived. Ted was in an animal shelter, which he avoided telling Meryl — Angela was unwell and unable to take care of Ted. Greg promised to check in on Ted at the shelter from time to time.

A media troupe was prowling on the walkway near the taxi drop-off point at the airport.

Marcia said, 'Oh something must be going on here today.'

Cameras clicked frenetically as Michael stepped out of the taxi and lights were flashed in Marcia's face,

'Ms Ntuli, are you pleased that the workplace harassment law in this country has been revamped?'

'Ms Ntuli, are you and Michael Morrissey more than just 'client and lawyer' with this trip to South Africa?'

Marcia was horrified that her trip with Michael had been leaked to the media. She knew she had to reply to avoid further speculation on her relationship status with him. She had to control her rising stress. Michael looked at her, his eyes forbidding her to say anything.

She regained her composure, 'I am pleased, as you can well imagine that workplace harassment is now given serious due diligence. Mr Morrissey is visiting South Africa to offer legal aid to people in need from my homeland. Thank you.'

They hurried off as voices called out behind them, 'Mr Morrissey... any comment... one more question Ms Ntuli ...'

They both fell into their seats on board SAA 2010, relieved that they escaped the onslaught of further questions.

'I cannot believe how well you handled the media, Marcia, I was quite seriously, weak in the knees! How on earth did they know we were flying out today? By the way I know you threw that in, but, I would love to offer legal aid in South Africa if it were at all possible.'

Don't worry about that now, I want you to see South Africa through my eyes, to feel the spirit of *Ubuntu*.

*   *   *

They enjoyed the relaxing, twelve hour flight. *OR Tambo Airport* in Johannesburg was bustling like most major airports around the world much to Michael's surprise.

The friendly, almost casual attitude of staff as they checked out created an air of laid back joviality to a foreigner.

'Wow, I can already feel the vibrancy of the place.'

'Easy now Michael, like all big cities, you have to be cautious in all matters, a friendly face can be deceptive so proceed with care or ask before you err,' Marcia laughed.

'Will do Miss Marcia, that 'teacher voice' means business, I get it!'

Two young men ran up to them offering to assist with their

bags while trying to strike up a conversation, in Xhosa with Marcia.

'You must speak English, ok, I have an English speaking friend with me who is a visitor to our country so we must speak English to include him, please.'

The young men smiled saying, '*Eish* sorry *sissie*,' as they turned to Michael and offered a South African handshake, 'Welcome to South Africa!'

Marcia's 'proceed with caution' look made Michael say little as he hurried along to the taxi.

Both young men smiled and hurried behind him,

'We can help you to your taxi for a few bob, ok?'

Michael loved the fresh enthusiasm with which the young men wanted to make him feel welcome with the local handshake and offers of assistance 'for a few bob.'

Marcia tipped them as they boarded the taxi to the hotel in the city of Sandton.

The luxurious top end accommodation, was a close walk to *Mandela Square* where the 6-metre bronze statue of Nelson Mandela stood tall, erect and smiling.

Once they had unpacked and freshened up they headed to the coffee shop downstairs to chat about Marcia's plans for them in Johannesburg. Michael was accustomed to Meryl's choices in their lives and accepted that Marcia would do the same. The level of trust between them led to this day where Michael placed the next few weeks totally in Marcia's hands.

'Michael, you know that crime is rife in this country and there is the beautiful spirit of the people and the land. No doubt a land of contrasts, contradictions and lovely weather. While I will be around to caution you, somewhat like your tour guide,' she laughed, 'please be mindful and vigilant at all times. Your upbringing makes you carefree and trusting of people, but as a native of this land, I can boldly say, we both have to be vigilant about safety. In saying that I do not mean to make you uneasy, I really do want you to take in the entire experience as you have been passionate about visiting South Africa for a long time now.'

'Thanks Marcia, I appreciate your honesty and will heed your advice. I saw the warning message card in my apartment with the cautionary advice about being vigilant especially at night.'

'In my childhood days, crime was virtually absent, many years of injustice, unemployment and other social dynamics ate away at the soul of the people which has led to this. I will never justify crime but have an understanding of why this is as it is. The beauty is, all people, regardless of race and ethnicity are free to associate with each other now and can live and work where they choose to.'

Michael knew that they would be having dinner with Ameera Simons, Marcia's friend from her university days and her family the next evening, at their home in a nearby suburb.

'You will enjoy meeting Ameera and Ian, as I mentioned on the flight, she is now a high school principal and Ian runs a few restaurants in this area. Ameera insisted on preparing a home-cooked meal for us.'

'That's really gracious of her, I look forward to meeting them. If I travelled here alone I would not have the five star 'insider' experience I will be getting by being here with you.'

'You do not have to be indebted to me for anything, kind sir! This is easy for me, you wanted to visit South Africa, our paths connected. I am indebted to you for giving me a renewed belief in myself, this has made me want to continue living and working abroad– you made me realise that a beautiful land like yours with loving, giving people should not be marred by my experience.'

Michael smiled, warmed by Marcia's belief that she mattered enough to return to the place she had come to love, his country, now, her home.

'We should toss the heavy stuff,' he said, 'and enjoy the experience together.'

*   *   *

Ameera and Ian lived in a gated community, where Marcia and Michael had to sign in at the gatehouse before they were allowed to enter the property. The gatehouse supervisor was a pleasant man, explaining that he had to call the Simons to let them know their guests had arrived.

Marcia's cautionary words began to make sense as Michael absorbed the necessity for security measures in residential suburbs.

The dinner with Ameera and Ian was an experience Michael enjoyed. The warmth of their home and love they showed Marcia had him basking in the joy of their reunion.

No questions were asked about how they met, it was quietly accepted that Michael was a close friend of Marcia's which made him more welcome in their home. Ian mentioned that he and Ameera would never have been allowed to marry, let alone have a relationship, under the old dispensation. He indicated that while they made their own decision to marry, they had to face questions from their families on both sides. Ian was Jewish, Ameera was fourth generation Indian; both families had grave reservations about this union, with the added baggage of apartheid alive for some. Ian revealed that all are united in great joy now after a few cautionary years before their families came together. Their children were part of two rich cultures, embraced by love without the shadow of racial difference. He said his children were fortunate to learn the value of *Chesid* and *Daya* which he explained was Hebrew for loving-kindness and Hindi for compassion.

Michael understood that hardship under apartheid brought a profound need to uplift the human condition for the next generation.

Listening to their recollections of forbidden love under a newborn post-apartheid sky made Michael grateful for his carefree youth, where nothing mattered apart from the next thrill as a young man. He studied Ian, seeing that as a white male growing up in South Africa, he had wholeheartedly embraced the disbanding of apartheid.

Michael listened to Ian's belief that 'nobody could replace Nelson Mandela as leader with the same sense of morality and selfless justice.'

Marcia looked at the two men in earnest conversation and was satisfied that Michael was comfortable and above all accepted with warmth and love.

Chapter 16

A very honest woman but something given to lie
Shakespeare — Anthony and Cleopatra

~

The media outside the courtroom on that imminent Monday morning made Meryl uneasy. Ben would have been horrified with the pushing crowd and invasive media at the courthouse.

It was clear that Ana's final words in Friday's hearing had rippled through the community, curiosity got the better of the public who wanted to hear first-hand about the life and times of Professor Andrei Malakov.

The judge was agitated that people were thronging in at 10 am. He ordered the door to be shut to avoid further loss of time.

*   *   *

Meryl left Alec undisturbed to digest the outcome of Friday's proceedings.

He called her on Saturday morning to meet later that day. Meryl was nervous, unsure if she was up to any further surprises. She pondered whether Alec had knowledge of Ana's claims.

A subdued Alec sat alone waiting for Meryl. He picked a table at the furthest end of the café for obvious privacy.

'I'm so glad to see you Meryl, how have you been?'

'Ok thank you, Alec,' she lied. 'Ben and I spent a quiet Friday evening together, I popped in to see Andrei this morning; Dr Spartan indicated he was improving. How are you doing, Alec?'

'Yes, I'm stoked that Andrei is improving. I would be more relieved when he is able to walk and talk, the slipping in and out of a coma has been distressing me, and the revelation at Friday's hearing was shattering to say the least. I know Boris and Andrei were not close but to hear that there is a possibility that Boris is not Andrei's son, well, I don't know what to believe anymore. I feel like a voyeur into the secret life of my childhood.'

'I know Alec, this was an unexpected bolt out the blue, for sure. Is Ana's revelation legitimate, or is she trying to stir things up because she is protecting Boris? What does she have to gain from this? If this is true, like you, Andrei is unaware of such claims.'

'I don't know to be honest. Andrei being the principled man he is, chose not to poison me against my mother or grandparents. I know, he was not happy with my grandfather's treatment of staff. I was aware as I grew older that he went his way as my mother's allegiance to her father excluded him. I really have no memory of ever being a 'family' together with Andrei and my mother and her family. Boris and I did not grow up as siblings should, there is no bond whatsoever between us. Who knows, I'm really confused by it all.'

'Well, vindication across time is all we can hope for, I suppose, the truth shall prevail for both you and Andrei. Lord knows what else might be sprung by Ana on Monday. She either says nothing most of the time and now says too much. I don't feel comfortable at all how this trial is unfolding.'

'Yes, it's a waiting game but I fear I don't have nerves of steel for this. I believe Gildo Mondo will want to see us at some point again with this coming to light, I don't know if I can bear hearing what Boris is going to say. Brad has to return to New York, next week, his work pressure is mounting and as much as he insists on staying, I told him to go back and attend to his business. God knows how long this is going take before we know where we all stand.'

*   *   *

Ana walked, with her regular, statuesque, stiff, gait to continue with what was left unfinished on Friday.

The prosecutor summed up Friday's session and began with further questions,

'Ms Kuznetsov, your claim that Boris Malakov is not Andrei Malakov's son needs to be supported with how you acquired this information as Boris Malakov's birth certificate states that his father is indeed Andrei Malakov.'

Ana was silent for a long time, she knew she could not stop what she had already started.

'I have this information directly from my mother who was aware that my father was having an affair with Miss Mariya for many years. She said he never denied it but always asked her not to bring up such things, until one day when he was quite ill, he told her that Boris was really his son and they had to be quiet about it as they needed the extra money from Mariya and her father.'

'Don't you think, Ms Kuznetsov, that your mother might have said this in a moment of anger? We have no proof to support this claim except that it makes Boris Malakov appear guilty in Professor Malakov's shooting which makes your claim a heavy one. The question raised now, is, why would you expose Boris this way if he truly is your brother?'

'I am telling the truth sir as I am expected to in this court of law, this is the truth as I know it. My intention is not to expose Boris as anything other than my much-loved half-brother. I do not believe he would attempt to kill his stepfather.'

'I see, does Boris Malakov know that the professor is not his biological father?'

'Yes he does, my father had a private conversation with him before he passed on, my mother said it was to tell him the truth.'

'Were you aware that there was a plot afoot to harm Professor Malakov?'

'No sir.'

'You were involved in the abduction of Ms Moorecroft, were you not?'

Ana was silent again, she looked across at Meryl who froze under her emotionless stare.

'I did not know Ms Moorecroft was going to be kidnapped. I only realised it was her, when Boris asked me to come to the place where she was held 'to look after someone' for him he said.'

'You did not think to ask who you would be looking after, Ms Kuznetsov. Did you not think it was unusual that someone was being held hostage and you were asked to 'look after' that 'someone'?'

The judge coughed, looked across at Ana Kuznetsov, in a cocked, half slant, left-sided view, like a bird on its perch, anticipating her response.

'No, Boris did not like being asked too many questions so I accepted to assist with no questions.'

'Pardon me, so if you were asked by Boris Malakov to murder someone, I take it you will do it without asking any questions because he did not like being asked questions, Ms Kuznetsov?'

This time the judge raised his voice,

'Proceed without badgering the witness!'

'May I, please proceed, your Honour? I'm trying to establish what power and control Boris Malakov had over Ms Kuznetsov.'

'Rephrase your question,' barked the judge.

'Did Boris Malakov seem demanding to you Ms Kuznetsov?'

'I did not see it as demanding, more my duty as an older sibling, by many years, to assist whenever I could.'

'Let the records show that Boris Malakov had a demanding attitude,' the prosecutor instructed.

'Sir, as Russians we stick by our families in any situation; that is what my father would have expected of me. He told me to watch over Boris, he was a lost child, he said.'

Horror filled Meryl's mind, 'what if Andrei had died when he was shot? What if he does not pull through? Would she and Alec ever know whether Andrei was aware that Boris was not his son?' A small part of her admired Ana's steadfast allegiance to her half-brother.

The judge called for a half-hour adjournment. He urged those present to be prompt in returning to their seats.

*   *   *

Meryl and Alec heard Inspector Aldo call out to them as they walked out onto the street.

'Ms Moorecroft, Mr Malakov, how are you two bearing up in all of this? I recommend you stay indoors, the media will pounce on you at any time.'

Meryl looked at the inspector in disbelief, wondering what he had eaten for breakfast to have become considerate!

'We are shocked at what has transpired but have to continue in strength for Andrei and Alec.'

The sheepish look on the inspector's face convinced Meryl

that he was out sniffing for more that he invariably would feed to the media being the cunning fox he was!

'Alec and I will head back now, thank you for your concern, Inspector Aldo.'

'That man is incorrigible, Alec! We have to be one step ahead of him. He has more power than he lets on. He pulls the strings in this town, too much that has become public knowledge is not coincidence.'

'I am inclined to agree. Andrei, when he did reveal anything, was not happy that his social gatherings at the villa often brought the inspector to his door enquiring about the nature of the social event.'

Meryl expected members of the public to have left after the brief recess — the courtroom remained packed to capacity.

Dmitri Repin was recalled to the stand in an attempt to clarify Ana's testimony regarding Boris Malakov.

'Mr Repin, you know you have been recalled to confirm your association and knowledge of Boris Malakov's involvement in the shooting of Professor Malakov.'

'I have told you all I know, sir.'

'Yes, now we need to establish whether you knew that Boris Malakov was not the biological son of Professor Malakov — is this your understanding Mr Repin?'

'Staff did talk about the madam and the chauffeur, Ms Kuznetsov's father — staff talk sir, I did not pay too much attention. The boy stayed at his grandfather's house which is not odd in our culture.'

'Tell the court what you knew of Boris Malakov's involvement in the abduction of Ms Moorecroft and the subsequent shooting of the professor.'

'Boris sent me an email before he arrived, saying he wanted

me to locate three men for him and to tell them to contact him urgently.'

'Who were these people Mr Repin?'

'I don't know them personally, sir, they seemed to have met Mr Boris before.'

'What makes you say that Mr Repin?'

'When I found them, one of them said, 'what is Boris up to now?' which made me think they worked with him or knew him well.'

'On the night that Ms Moorecroft was aware that someone was in the villa ransacking the professor's study, she sent you a text message for help, why did you not reply to her?'

'I did not receive any message from Ms Moorecroft.'

'Mr Repin our investigation reveals that the message was received by you and deleted.'

Dmitri sat silent like a boy hauled in by the school headmaster.

'Mr Repin, did you delete the message?'

Silence.

'The court requires your answer Mr Repin,' the judge ordered.

Silence.

'Yes, I did.'

'Why did you delete the message, the professor left you to assist Ms Moorecroft while he was out of the country? Please explain why you ignored her cry for help.'

'Mr Boris told me he knew there was a woman, an English woman, staying at the villa with his father and that I was to take her back to the apartment in Florence — he did not want her at the villa that night.'

Meryl felt agitated as she recalled that awful night, she remembered Boris referring to her as 'you English' when he was angered by her many questions while she was being held hostage, stifling her attempt to correct him that she was not English.

'Why was Ms Moorecroft still at the villa on the night of her abduction?'

Meryl was glad Ben was not present, this would have been unbearable for him to hear first-hand that her cry for help was ignored.

'I could not ask her to leave when I picked Ana up because Professor Malakov said Ms Meryl was not to be disturbed as she was busy working at the villa,' Dmitri said.

'Were you aware that Boris was going to raid the villa on that fateful day?'

'No sir, I did not know the details of his plans. I found the men for him and then had nothing further to do with it sir, please believe me.' He begged like a helpless child caught in a situation where all fingers pointed at him.

'Did you go to the location where Ms Moorecroft was being held?'

'No sir, I was here, in Florence working.'

'Why did you leave Florence when news broke that the professor had been shot?'

'I was scared, I had nothing to do with it. All I did was find the men Boris asked me to find.'

The session was adjourned for the day and recalled for 1:30 pm the next day.

Meryl felt the late start might be to uncover more information that would be used in the next hearing.

Chapter 17

And thus I clothe my naked villainy
With odd old ends stol'n out of holy writ
And seem a saint, when most I play the devil.
Shakespeare — Richard III

~

Meryl's hurried walk to the police station to see Inspector Aldo was an unplanned diversion on her way to the hospital.

She was in the corridor on her way up to Aldo's office which was situated on the second floor when she stopped dead in her tracks — a voice on the stairwell was unmistakably of one of the men who held her hostage in the van. She peered from behind a downstairs wall — there was Inspector Aldo, grinning like a malicious Cheshire cat in friendly banter with two men who were not visually familiar to her. The red-haired man's voice was a distinct recollection for her, his laugh was that of the voice that sneered at her when she asked to go to the toilet.

Her mind raced, *why was Inspector Aldo talking to these men who were allowed to leave? Why did he appear to be very friendly with them?*

She waited until both men walked down the stairs and into

the reception area before she ran up calling out, 'Inspector Aldo, may I have a minute please.' He spun around, surprised to see her. His usual mocking eyes were now wide open, his voice, out of character in its softness,

'Everything ok Ms Moorecroft, has something happened to Professor Malakov? To what do I owe this unannounced visit?'

'Yes, much the same as when I last saw you, I would imagine. I was on my way to the hospital and decided I would stop to check if you had any news on the men who took me from the villa. I am uneasy that they are still at large, inspector.' She studied his face for any tell-tale signs of guilt.

This was not what she had intended to see the inspector about, but, this prickly opportunity presented itself to test and perhaps confirm her suspicions of the inspector once and for all. She thought she saw the colour rise a tad in his cheeks. She wished she could record his response.

His voice was now composed, his grating tone returned,

'No news, the search is still out, Mr Repin has provided the details of the identity of the men he was asked to find for Boris Malakov. How is the professor doing?' *Clever diversion,* she thought.

'I am on my way to see him as I said, so no update just yet. Will you let me know when they are found so that I can sleep easy again?' Meryl looked for further signs of guilt or a hint that he knew more than he was letting on. He resumed his aloof manner.

'I will Ms Moorecroft, I have some calls to make and I do encourage you to call and book a time to see me rather than turn up like you have this evening.'

'Yes, I saw two men with you, you must have had a meeting; I'm sorry inspector, I'll be sure to call in future to forewarn you.'

Inspector Aldo maintained his sneering countenance of dark hidden secrets.

*   *   *

Alec was rubbing Andrei's hands in soft, slow strokes, leaning over as if in conversation with him when Meryl walked in.

Meryl touched Andrei's hands to indicate her presence and motioned to Alec to step out the room with her.

'Alec, I'm really troubled by what I saw as well as heard this evening when I stopped over to see Inspector Aldo at the police station.'

What is it? Why did you go down to see him alone? He is a dangerous man! What's happened that's disturbed you this way?'

'As I approached the stairway to head up to Aldo's office, I heard him talking to two men outside his office, sort of an end of meeting conversation, I think. The thing is, the voice of the red-haired man, I am convinced, is the voice of one of the men that held me hostage in the van. I can't be sure about the other mousey-haired man, he did not speak and as I was blindfolded I cannot verify who he is. The red-head is one of them — Aldo was in a very 'chummy' conversation with them and let them leave.'

'Did you mention that to Inspector Aldo? Something is so perverse in all of this Meryl and we have no one to turn to for advice here. It's like navigating an elusive maze to get to the truth.'

'He was flustered for a moment when he saw me but regained his brittle composure — he told me never to come to his office without an appointment. I told him I saw two men leaving his office. He has no idea I heard part of the conversation.'

'Gee Meryl, you should not be strolling around at night, your abductors are out and about in close proximity, around us and we have no idea who they are. We should speak to Gildo Mondo, I think we need legal counsel now.'

'Ben does not know that I stopped off at the station, please keep this between us for now, I really don't want to stress him — he has grave reservations regarding Inspector Aldo's agenda in this case. I agree we should give Gildo Mondo a call soon. You may tell Brad about tonight, that's ok. We should go in to sit with Andrei.'

That night Alec accompanied Meryl back to her hotel for another set of eyes around, should anyone approach her. He knew he would not be able to protect her if they were accosted by any of these men.

Meryl thought of sending Michael a text message about the events of the evening– she realised that Inspector Aldo might have already put a tap on her phone. She decided to avoid any legal ramifications and sent him a polite text message asking after him and Marcia and how things were going in South Africa.

Ben was awake watching BBC news when she checked in on him.

'Everything ok Meryl? You look so tired darling. I'm watching this Brexit fiasco, everything is falling apart these days.'

'You can say that again, I just want this over, I want Andrei to recover, if he chooses to go back to his old life and never see me again, I will accept that. I have to see this through, I still don't know where all this is leading to. Did Boris order the ransom? Was he working alone or as a syndicate with others? Who knows? I am more worried than I am worn out actually.'

'Have you had any news from Michael, how are things in South Africa? The news seems to highlight all things negative globally these days. Reminds of these lines my dear, from Charles Dickens' in *A Tale of Two Cities*, 'It was the best of times, it was the worst of times...'

'I miss our literary tête-à-têtes, soon, hopefully this will be behind us... soon I hope. I feel awful about deserting you these days.'

'Not at all my dear, that's what family is all about, through thick and thin, there will be time yet to pick up our literary duels.'

She said a thankful goodnight for his constant love, the only constant thing in her life with no judgements and recriminations.

Chapter 18

Poise the cause in justice's equal scales, whose beam
stands sure, whose rightful cause prevails.
Shakespeare — Henry IV, Part 2

~

The visit to the apartheid museum in Johannesburg was a chilling one for Michael who chose to go in twice, first through the 'whites only' gate for the white experience under apartheid rule, then he stepped in with Marcia through the 'non-whites' entrance. The photographs, archival footage and surreal flashback to that inhumane time left Marcia a little emotional. They sat outside in the sun not a word between them, absorbing the experience which would live with Michael for a long time to come.

'I'm sorry for becoming emotional, Michael, memories came gushing back of the days when Mama Dolores was under suspicion and the police would barge into our home in the middle of the night and drag her to the police station for questioning. They were so rough with her, they broke things in the house and booted things down as they stomped through the house, kicking her in the back calling her an *evil kaffir*. It was horrible. The neighbour would have to watch over me when mama was taken. She would return the next day, bedraggled, swollen-faced and silent for days on end, the sadness about her would eventually lift — it had to, the young woman she cared for, needed her. She did nothing but promote literacy which the local Irish priest supported. He spoke to the police about the content of Mama Dolores' character and her work with the women and her commitment to the church but it always fell on deaf ears. It was a painful, dark time in our history. Because I was witness to the atrocities, it lives close, under my skin, if you know what I mean.'

'I can understand why your emotions resurface Marcia. I am beginning to see things through your eyes, many will not comprehend the dehumanising impact of this regime much like the time of slavery and the stolen generation — nothing can erase the pain of such suffering as it has been said, 'a history forgotten is a future lost.' Memory will live on to pave the way for a better future. You *must* not forget, you *must* keep telling your story, it's the only way to awaken the next generation to what is bestial and in need of quashing. Let's sit here for a while longer.

Marcia remained subdued for the rest of that day.

*   *   *

The next day, Ian's driver, Jabu, took them on a tour through Soweto, which had gone through several transformations. Some of the country's great musicians emerged from Soweto making great contributions to the voice of the people. Marcia's childhood friend, Portia, lived in Soweto. Her family still lived there but she had moved to Cape Town to work as a legal secretary. Marcia planned to see her when they were in Cape Town. Jabu acted as a patient tour guide, explaining in great detail to Michael, that the Soweto he was seeing now had changed.

There was improvement, people felt more settled and happy although poverty still hung over them. Michael saw groups of young men on street corners, dancing and laughing, little informal markets where fruit and vegetables were displayed and sold with pride. Large, flimsy wire cages held agitated fowls whose beady eyes peered with suspicion whenever people approached. Marcia explained that a 'live' fowl instead of a frozen one was considered a delicacy. Young women walked along the poorly drained streets after the previous night's rain calling out in rhythmic chant,

'Carpet brooms, good brooms, strong brooms, cheap-cheap brooms. Carpet brooms, good brooms, strong brooms, cheap-cheap brooms.'

Enterprising young women were trying to make an honest living for their families from the grass brooms they wove. The colourful experience had Michael journaling profound moments on his iPad. He only photographed that which moved him. He was not a tourist. He was here to experience people, culture and history. A little cuisine was not lost on him either.

Lunch was a treat of *samp and beans* which Marcia called staple 'soulful' food. Jabu explained that the fibre in such a meal sustained workers who often had to travel long distances to work in the cities or work with tremendous physicality on the mines. The vibrant spirit of the people put Michael at ease after Marcia's cautionary comments on safety. As they headed back to the vehicle, a group of young girls loitered around looking at Marcia with curious admiration, one of them chirped,

'Hey *si'ssie* you a coconut? You got nice clothes, designer brand! Wow!'

'Hello ladies, I am just like you, not a coconut and you can have nice clothes too when you finish your studying and start working. These are not designer clothes. How old are you?'

'We are sixteen and in grade ten, we're studying hard so we

can go overseas one day and work and get nice clothes.' They laughed mimicking walking in stiletto heels, up on tip toes.

'I'm so happy to hear you are in school, you can achieve your dreams with hard work, let nobody take that away from you. Look after yourselves, do not be in a great hurry to get married ok?'

'Thank you, but if a rich man, like yours comes, we must take the offer.' They laughed again with provocative glances in Michael's direction.

Jabu laughed as the girls walked away, 'How did you feel being called a *coconut* Marcia?'

'What that does that refer to?' Michael asked.

Marcia laughed so much, tears streamed down her cheeks, 'they saw you, Michael, and assumed I was trying to be white too, you know a coconut, dark on the outside and white on the inside? There was a television show here called, *The Coconuts*, you should watch it, it might make greater sense why the term becomes applicable in a post-apartheid South Africa.'

Michael could not help but say, 'Well Ms Ntuli, 'I do declare, *you are* a coconut after all!'

That set Marcia and Jabu off into more fits of laugher, Jabu's booming laugh had people looking at them as they walked past sending lots of smiles in their direction.

Michael felt the contradictions of this beautiful, vibrant and ravaged place, he looked forward to hearing the *Soweto Gospel Choir* at their fund-raiser concert in the city that night.

The exotic costumes, a flurry of red, purple, yellow, bright pink, deep blue, soft greys and browns complemented the baritone and alto blends which enthralled Michael. He glanced over at Marcia during the passionate, pleading, lyrical outpouring of *Amazing Grace*, tears rolled down her cheeks as she mouthed the words, alone in this vision and moment. Almost on cue, the room rose in a rhythmic swaying motion, eyes ablaze or closed in tight serenity, afraid to let go of the emotion, joy, suffering and pain merged in the euphoria of the moment. Michael had never before felt the thunderous vibration of human unison like he did on that night.

*   *   *

Meryl called Michael as he was settling down for the night. He and Marcia had separate apartments which gave him the privacy to speak to Meryl as Marcia intended.

'Hi Michael, how are things going in South Africa?'

'Meryl, so far it has been an experience that will remain etched in the memory bank, it would have been good had we carried out our plans to make South Africa our next tour destination. You will fall in love with the place and have so much to blog about. How are things going with the trial? Is Andrei showing signs of improving?'

'Wow it sounds like an awesome trip so far and how fortunate that you're travelling with a native South African. The trial gets more complicated with each testimony, but Andrei miraculously is showing signs of improving, the swelling around the brain has eased, Dr Spartan says once his heart rate is significantly stronger they will operate.'

'That's good news, Meryl, fingers crossed that all goes well with him. What are the complications that have emerged with the trial? Are you up to talking about it, or are you prohibited from discussing the case?'

'On the contrary, these are public hearings, so nothing is a secret really. The news each day begins with the trial and reporters are vultures at the door so don't be surprised if I turn up on the South African television news soon!' she managed to laugh. 'It has now been revealed that Boris is not the biological son of Andrei, this came as quite a shock to Alec so it will be good to hear what Andrei has to say about all this. Ana said she was the half-sister, her father is Boris' father.'

'Geez, Meryl, that's huge, poor Alec, surely things could not get any more complicated than that, although it indicates a quicker end in sight if Boris is indeed the bastard son out to kill his stepfather. Sounds like a Shakespearean tragedy, it's surreal to say the least. I'm sure you are contemplating blogging on this later.'

'Indeed, one would hope the end is in sight. Blogging? What's that Mike? I'm forbidden to post anything, the prime reason I came on this junket. I feel I'm living the Shakespearean tragedy, yes it would be great blogging content. Inspector Aldo, the cad, is doing something underhanded too, I feel it in my bones. I overheard him talking to two men the other night at the precinct, the one talking, sounded distinctly like one of my captors, from the night I was taken from the villa. I am in a quandary here. I don't know who to trust. Alec is the only one. He knows of my suspicions and suggested I speak to Andrei's attorney, Gildo Mondo. I don't know yet, is that such a good idea, you think? By the way, Ben knows nothing about my suspicion, he does not need any added stress. I really should not be speaking to you about the case, my phone could be tapped.'

Michael felt the pressure Meryl was under, she had called him, 'Mike' for the first in weeks and spoke almost in one long breathe like she had to release it all before the next shock hit her.

'Meryl, you need to report it, Gildo Mondo would be the best one to talk to as he represents Andrei so chances are he will support you and Alec. I will be glad once this is all over, your safety above all is my concern, promise you'll be careful.'

They parted on good terms that night. Michael was glad that Meryl was still comfortable to turn to him for advice.

The beautiful, melodious sounds of the 'a cappella harmony of the Soweto Gospel Choir remained with Michael, drawing him into a deep, hypnotic sleep.

Chapter 19

The first thing we do, let's kill all the lawyers.
Shakespeare — Henry VI, Part 2

~

The trial session that afternoon brought Gildo Mondo to the stand. Meryl knew she would be called soon regarding the night of her abduction.

Gildo Mondo walked up to the witness box with his customary world on his shoulders walk, pensive with eyes averted from the public gallery and media glare.

'Mr Mondo, you have been a close associate and legal advisor to Professor Malakov, is that right?' the prosecutor asked.

'In a legal capacity, that was the close association, we were not social friends, I need to clearly establish that.'

'Thank you for clarifying that. Explain why the professor came to Pelago to see you just prior to his departure to Russia.'

'He said he was going to finalise his divorce as his estranged wife was ailing and he wanted to review his will which he did. I did question him on the change he made, but he assured me he was of sound mind when he made that change.'

'Are you able to reveal to the court what that change was Mr Mondo?'

'No sir, I am bound by client confidentiality and cannot see how that information will shed more light on this case in any way?'

'As a legal man, as you are aware, you could be asked to reveal this at an 'in camera' hearing'

'Yes, yes if it's essential to serving due justice then I am under oath to do so if comment is to be made in a 'held in camera' session.'

'Do you have any knowledge of Mr Boris Malakov being a stepson to the professor?'

'No sir, that was not said to me although I am aware that Boris and the professor were not on good terms, for reasons I cannot divulge here, due to client confidentiality and that this is a public forum.'

'Did the professor reveal what his content was on his next *Time* magazine publication?'

'No, not the unpublished manuscript, but I was aware of his stance on child labour exploitation. He was vocal on this and rightfully so. I am at liberty to say he did seek legal counsel regarding his rights to report matters that were unjust'

'I see, one final question, how long have you known Professor Malakov?'

'From the time he purchased the villa in Viareggio, which is about some twenty or more years ago, he asked me to process the deed of sale and all legal encumbrances thereof and I have been his legal advisor ever since.'

'A long association, indeed. That will be all for now, you might be called again at a later stage.'

The judge called for a fifteen-minute recess asking the prosecutor to meet him upstairs.

Ben and Brad were in court with Meryl and Alec that afternoon. They stepped outdoors to mull over all they had just heard.

'Mondo seems reticent, don't you think Meryl? Alec asked. 'He knows something more about Andrei's article for *Time* than he is letting on. As the legal advisor would he not have cautioned Andrei if the article he was writing was courting danger?'

'I'm on that page too, Alec', Meryl answered. 'I think he indicated that Andrei checked out the legality regarding writing the article but could not advise him on personal grounds not to do so, he declares that they were not social associates. I wonder if we will ever get to know what Mondo reveals 'in camera' to the judge, wish I was a fly on the wall in that session. I'm beginning to feel the pressure of time; the legal system certainly drags its heels on some matters.'

Ben who had not said much today spoke up, 'We have to focus on the positives, Andrei is showing remarkable signs of recovery, we must keep that positive energy up — he must have a voice in all that has happened, his life was almost snuffed out, we shall have answers soon.'

Brad nodded throughout Ben's affirmation, 'Yes, Ben, while we both fully appreciate the weight that Alec and Meryl carry, we will pull through. Time will vindicate truth in due course.'

Alec had his world turned inside out with Andrei's shooting and Ana's revelation that Boris was not his father's son — his half-brother. It was enough in a short space of time to drive anyone over the edge.

They walked back into the courtroom optimistic with the wisdom Ben and Brad brought to their little group.

*   *   *

Inspector Aldo strode in like the lord mayor himself, oozing arrogance from every pore. Unlike Gildo Mondo, he looked directly at the public gallery, basking in the attention of the media frenzy — clicking cameras, hurried pens writing page after page, not missing a moment of his *Ozymandias* countenance in his sculptured *sneer of cold command*.

'Inspector Aldo, you were the chief investigator appointed to the case on the kidnapping of Ms Moorecroft and the subsequent attack on Professor Malakov. Can you fill the court in on how you were alerted and how you proceeded with the investigation?' the prosecutor asked, looking up from his papers. His eyes were in view as he raised his fanned-out eyebrows in anticipation of the inspector's comment.

Meryl felt Ben's grip tighten on her arm.

'Certainly,' Inspector Aldo said as he looked around the courtroom in a slow panning movement, 'I was alerted by Interpol as Ms Moorecroft's partner raised the alarm bell when she could not be reached for a couple of days. I acted on instruction and followed through from there.'

'Was Professor Malakov known to you, Inspector?'

'Oh yes, his frequent arrivals and departures in Florence, in the present political climate made him one to be followed by a watchful eye.'

'Was there any reason other than his departures and arrivals that made him a person of interest?'

'I daresay! He held large social gatherings at the villa, it is a secluded estate where suspicion of improper conduct prevails.'

'So you had no legal or binding reason for having Professor Malakov on your radar other than his frequent trips to Florence and his social life that you deemed suspicious?'

The inspector paused, his calculating stare did not deter the prosecutor who looked back unblinking, eyebrows raised almost to his hairline as he stood waiting for Inspector Aldo's response.

The judge interjected, 'Answer the questor inspector.'

'Well yes and no.'

'You need to be more specific sir.'

'He was a silent man, you know, not the buoyant person as *we* Italians are, he was aloof which made me feel he was hiding something.'

'As a police officer, one who heads the precinct, should you be basing your judgements on 'feelings' and 'assumptions' rather than facts, Inspector?

The judge called an objection which stroked the inspector's lofty ego, adding more to his already obnoxious arrogance.

'Did you know Professor Malakov was a great contributor to the Arts and Literary Council here, that he is a generous contributor to raising adult literacy in Italy and the children's orphanage?'

'Yes, I am aware of his contributions. Often those *who want to be seen* doing the most for others, have the most to hide is my understanding.'

'Your personal views are not solicited in this courtroom, Inspector Aldo, keep to the facts,' the prosecutor hissed through clenched teeth.

Meryl smiled for the first time in many days, enjoying witnessing the inspector receiving a dose of his own crude medicine.

'When did you first meet Ms Moorecroft?'

'When we recovered her after the professor was shot, she ran out from the surrounding scrub when she heard the gunshots. I spoke to her much later after the professor was hospitalised.'

'Did she cooperate with you in your investigation on the shooter?'

'She did, she did. I can't say the same for Dr Hart, her family member.'

Meryl felt the heat rising to her cheeks, why did the darned inspector have to bring Ben's name up when he had nothing to do with any of this! She struggled to remain composed, her clammy palms let go of Ben's consoling hand.

'Dr Hart?'

'Yes, her uncle, he came in from London with Ms Moore-croft's partner, Mr Morrissey, a human rights lawyer in his country. Mr Morrissey was compliant, but Dr Hart was non-committal except when he flew off the handle regarding Ms Moorecroft's reputation — very strange indeed.'

'Let's keep to the case Inspector. Ms Moorecroft and her family are not suspects in this case.'

'It just seems strange, his behaviour I mean.' Inspector Aldo had the gall to look directly at Ben as he made this comment which the prosecutor saw as a ploy to scatter his line of questioning. Inspector Aldo was attempting to take the heat off himself by coming out in full attack first of Andrei and now Ben.

'How well do you know Boris Malakov?'

'I don't really know much about him, just about the brawl on the street one night when he was in Florence.'

'You dismiss that lightly inspector, yet the professor is the one you have held under suspicion.'

'Young men will drink, become irrational, that does not make them criminals. It's white collar crime that needs to be watched sir!'

Inspector Aldo continued with his need to drive fabricated nails into Andrei's coffin. The strange, elusive protection of Boris Malakov, confirmed that the inspector was in over his head in this case.

He would have quite a task to squirm his way out of this.

His ship was slowly sinking.

Chapter 20

I like this place and could willingly waste my time in it.
Shakespeare — As You Like It

~

The Cape shoreline was stunning, beautiful beaches, weather made for outdoor lifestyles, people with sunny, colourful dispositions proved a mind-blowing contrast from Soweto for Michael.

'Cape Town could be any place in the world, the Waterfront feels like the waterways at home,' Michael exclaimed.

'It's a beautiful part of South Africa and features prominently on the preferred holiday destinations even for native South Africans. You will love *The Kaapse Klopse* which is the cultural Minstrel Carnival here. That's held on Sunday, you are in for an experience of a lifetime, Michael!'

'I can't wait Marcia, being here has made me realise what a staid life I've been living. The experience so far is one I know I will always treasure.'

Marcia looked up at Michael and smiled, 'that makes me so happy. Seeing you relish it all, is *amazing* for me, it adds to my appreciation of home.' She stood up on tip toe and planted a kiss firmly on his mouth.

Michael was not expecting this show of affection. Marcia had become distant, not allowing intimacy between them ever since Meryl's disappearance in Florence. He felt relieved that she was more relaxed now.

He was a patient man. He would wait for the right moment.

'Come along we have a bit further to walk along the beach-way. You have to try some tasty beach morsels, 'chilli pineapple and *braaied mealies* –barbecued corn oozing with hot butter — *mmm* Michael it's the best!'

'Look at the foodie you are! You have my mouth watering for those treats! I figure, in for a penny, in for a pound, I can hit the gym again when I get back home,' he laughed as he put his arm around her shoulders.

'I love the Cape, we did not visit often but when we did, Mama Dolores always ensured it was very special.'

Sweet, salty, hot and pungent collided, tantalising Michael's tastebuds which Marcia assured him he would miss when he got back home. She told him he had to taste a bit of the *Kaapse snoek* to take his delectation for fish to a whole new level.

They spent the afternoon savouring tasty morsel after tasty morsel along the beach.

*   *   *

The Kaapse Klopse on Sunday exploded on the streets in an array of colour, exotic costumes, umbrellas in a sea of red, green and blue bobbed around to the sounds of strumming banjos, drum-beats, trumpets blaring with intermittent bursts of the sharp sound of a whistle punctuating the crescendo of sounds. The crowd clapped and cheered with smiles that stretched to the top of Table Mountain — such was the joy and harmony as the troupes made their way through the streets. This was the

Rainbow Nation Marcia referred to. The Cape Coloured experience had Michael swaying to the rhythmic sounds. Looking at Marcia revelling in this moment, reminded Michael of the night he saw her as band conductor at the school that threatened and discredited her pain. Her healing had come, she was stronger now and would contribute to the world with her wholesome and authentic connections to others.

Their last day was spent at the top of Table Mountain after an exhilarating cable car ride. The view was breath-taking. Michael contemplated this land of contradictions, such beauty and rarity were untouched, yet, dwelling deep in the souls of generations past and present was the corrosive memory of apartheid atrocities.

*   *   *

The flight to Durban was a short one.

Michael noticed the cosmopolitan landscape in Cape Town and Johannesburg. Durban had a dense population of Indian people, some were still living in the Group Areas racially demarcated suburbs. Marcia indicated that these were now more diverse suburbs. Parts of Durban looked like India, with its spice shops, saree and fabric stores, jewellery shops, Indian sweet shops and restaurants galore.

Marcia said there was a restaurant called, *The Goodwill Lounge* owned by a pioneering Indian family. Up and coming indigenous musicians and jazz artists launched their careers at that restaurant. The proprietors were notable social figures who offered top notch restaurant service and fine dining to all non-white patrons who were denied access to white owned restaurants. They also promoted sportsmen who wanted to break out into the boxing world. Whenever Mama Dolores and members of the church congregation travelled to Natal for inter-provincial meetings, they stopped at the *Goodwill Lounge* for a meal. She recalled her mother saying that it felt like being in a world where she had nothing to fear. She could be who she wanted to be in those carefree hours, savouring scrumptious curries and succulent Sunday roasts on the many trips there. She enjoyed being a lady on those visits, not a woman of colour who was constantly watched for speaking her truth, harming no one while she served those in need.

'I remember a time when a few friends and I wanted to dine at a beachfront restaurant to celebrate the 21st birthday of my friend Radha, we rang the restaurant to ask if non-white patrons were allowed in their restaurant, we did not expect to be allowed in, so that was a memorable night to say the least. Lots of curious glances came our way but staff treated us as respected fee-paying clients and that's all that mattered. That was a great night for Radha who lived in an orphanage all her life. She is a teacher at a high school here in Durban. She is away on a family holiday which is a pity as she has heart wrenching tales to tell of her life experience. There may be another time when you might be able to meet her. I'll make enquiries about her return. Our next stop will be Pietermaritzburg which is not a long way off from Durban.'

Marcia enjoyed sharing her stories with Michael, he was an engaged, enthralled listener who saved his questions to the end. She recalled wanting to spend a long weekend with her girlfriends on the North Coast of Durban. She called in to book a sea-facing room and enquired about breakfast and dining facilities at the hotel only to be told, non-whites were not allowed in the dining area, gas stoves and fridges were available in the rooms in the non-white section where they could cook, *'whatever you want, ok'* the receptionist said. Marcia thanked the lady saying if that was the situation it would not be a weekend away.

This attitude flummoxed Michael who was untouched by racism as Angela ensured she raised him and his sister Michelle to respect all people through tolerant understanding. He chose friends like Greg, his business partner who shared his values.

Ameera and her husband Ian had also urged Michael to be aware of petty crime in Durban which they said was more widespread than Johannesburg. Marcia hated being cautious about crime saying she preferred Cape Town where she felt one could have a semblance of freedom. He had not felt any of the concerns they drew his attention to, his free and open acceptance seemed to buffer him against any negative situations.

He was disturbed by the poverty and living conditions of informal settlements on the outskirts of Durban. He knew that corruptive politics and the legacy of apartheid would take a long time to clear the way, to end poverty through education by providing more opportunities for youth to rise to their true station in life. Marcia said Nelson Mandela had done much to improve the lot of the human condition for race groups. He kept rogue politicians in check. His passing had left the people unsure of their future as the gravy train of politicians grew heavier.

Marcia recounted her days as a student in a casual job which extended her political consciousness beyond the confines of home.

'As a student, I worked during the school holiday and some weekends at a stationery store that sold schoolbooks. It was there that I learned more about the injustice of the education system for indigenous students, my people. While school books were provided by the state for White, Indian and Coloured students, Indigenous students had to buy their own text books. Entry had to be through the back end of the store so as not to disturb the more affluent shoppers at the front of the well-lit, carpeted store. This angers me to this day, that the people who had the least, often nothing, like my mama, were forced to pay for their children's books while those who could afford it, did not have to fork out a cent. Maths, Science and English were deemed unnecessary in Bantu Education but rather a curriculum on gardening and housekeeping — how to be a good domestic worker — was given priority. There are so many layers to the injustice of apartheid Michael, all might seem incomprehensible to you. On the bright-side so much has come from suffering and struggle, Nelson Mandela left a legacy that education is the key to freedom.'

Michael listened, with each revelation the memory of his beloved brother flooded back. He gave thanks for his mother's good sense and his father's foresight on where he should be educated and his choice to be a human rights lawyer. Marcia too had strong family values, her mother acted as both mother and father instilling the importance of rising above one's situation and assisting others in their time of need.

He understood why Marcia needed to work in a different country to broaden her mindscape, to enrich her soul and then perhaps return to her people to widen their horizons on life, if that was to be her life path.

He would never stand in the way of her dreams and life choices. He hoped that he was a part of her life choices in their foreseeable futures.

Chapter 21

~

Andrei was in surgery.

Dr Spartan went ahead as Andrei's vital signs and swelling around the internal bullet-point of penetration had receded.

Meryl's morning was stressful — she was summoned to testify on the events of the night of her abduction and her days in captivity. She was desperate to be at the hospital to receive first-hand news on Andrei's condition during the surgery and post-surgery. She mustered all the strength she could — she had to get through this to move things forward for Andrei, Alec and herself. The letter she received at her hotel added to her mounting stress. It simply stated,

Go back to your country. Leave this alone!

The message was typed and addressed to *Ms Meryl* c/o the Eden Hotel, the ivory coloured envelope was of a thick and durable quality. The concierge told her it came through the postal service. The post mark was *Florence*.

Alec urged Meryl to report the matter. She did not trust

Inspector Aldo, now that she was convinced he knew her abductors, one of them at least. Gildo Mondo had not cleared in her book of trust either. She was not comfortable with him. This was Meryl's Achilles' heel, trust had to be demonstrated before she shared her world. She was often thought of as unfriendly or anti-social and a snob. Ben pointed out this change in her, when she met Andrei and proceeded without her drawn out customary caution in testing the trust of newcomers. He was somehow different, in a way she could not explain to Ben or Michael. She considered telling Michael about the note she received in the mail — she could not disturb him with this while he was in South Africa. She was also aware that time had widened the space between them, she was not sure how he would react to this detail. She was unsure of so many things since Andrei's entry into her world. She could not help thinking how Ben would draw in Robert Frost's *The Road Not Taken* quoting the lines, '...knowing *how way leads onto way* — to define this juncture in her life. Her trip to Florence had created a lasting impression which she knew would have a ripple effect well into her future.

*   *   *

The prosecutor looked up at Meryl,

'Can you please tell the court what happened the night you were kidnapped?'

'I became aware around 2:45 am that there were sounds in the villa suggesting I was not alone, I stepped out onto the hallway and saw the light on in Andrei's study — the door was slightly ajar. I heard what seemed to be two male voices, both of which I was not familiar with. I stepped back into my room and sent Dmitri Repin a text message. I also heard one voice on the phone say that the drafts of the manuscript for *Time* magazine could not be found. That is all I remember until I was conscious again in the van which travelled on a loose graveled road.'

'Thank you Ms Moorecroft for that detailed recount. Now proceed briefly with information on your abductors leading up to your release on that fateful day Professor Malakov was shot. Are you okay to proceed, Ms Moorecroft?' Meryl was thankful for the humane consideration from the prosecutor. She had lost faith in the integrity of the justice system under Inspector Aldo. She would tell it like it was.

'Yes sir, I am good to go on. I was blindfolded so can only provide information on what I heard, there appeared to be two or three men that were on the road with me, I was given water and food. My feet were tied as were my hands, which were later released. The men ensured I had no idea of the location when we stopped. They did not want to be asked any questions. They became aggressive when I asked where I was and why I was taken.'

'When you say aggressive, Ms Moorecroft what exactly do you mean, was it physical or verbal abuse that you experienced?'

'I was tied as I said, I was not physically abused in the van just told to 'shut up' and not ask questions. The tone of voice was aggressive enough to suggest that these men could become violent, that's the way I interpreted it.'

'Go on.'

'I must have been sedated because I have no memory for how I got to the place I was held in, a cloaked figure, a woman, a tall figure, brought me water and meals.'

'Did you notice anything about the voices of the men that might suggest their nationality?'

'One spoke English but slipped into Russian when he was angered. The one voice who said he was Andrei's son was different to the one I heard in the truck. He too spoke English with a slight accent which could have been a Russian accent, I'm not absolutely sure.'

'Were you subjected to any violence, brutality while you were there?'

'Yes, I was slapped across the face, pushed to the ground and abuse was hurled whenever it was perceived that I was non-compliant. I asked the cloaked woman if she was Ana as I recognised her gait, stature and her hands which were not covered.' Meryl tried at every opportunity to lead the questioning to Ana's involvement in her abduction. She had to ensure that somebody listened to this, she knew her intuition would not lead her astray.

The judge broke in unexpectedly and called for a forty minutes recess.

Meryl was relieved to have a little time with Ben and Alec. She was concerned that questioning might lead to her revealing that she had received a threatening letter. She spoke to Alec late the night before, he told her not to hold back if this came up as he too would need police protection if her safety was threatened. They had to be careful around Ben when they spoke.

'Good to see you are composed Meryl, I was worried about you, you are doing well, darling.' Ben said.

'Yes Meryl, you are very clear about the events. I also have some news from the hospital. Andrei is going well and should be in recovery around 3 pm. Please don't worry, I'm keeping an eye on the situation.'

'Thank you, Alec! This makes me feel loads better. Soon Andrei will be able to clarify things. I can't wait to hear his voice again.'

Ben looked at Meryl, his dark eyes pensive, he knew Meryl had given her heart to the 'roving professor' she admired so much. He hoped that there would be no further surprises in store for her. She had to get back to her writing ambition to reclaim her life, unfettered by the problems that beset her.

'I'll come with you to the hospital this evening Meryl, it's been a while since I looked in on Andrei.'

'That will be good Ben, perhaps Brad will join us too Alec? Meryl asked.

'I am about to call him now, I'll see you and Ben back in the courtroom. Good luck with the next round of questions Meryl. See you soon. He kissed her on her cheek and walked off.

'What a lovely young man Meryl, I have since adjusted my earlier opinion of Andrei. If he single-handedly raised Alec to be this courteous and considerate young man, then he must be a fine man indeed.'

Meryl smiled, she needed Ben's approval of Andrei, far more than he realised. She was nervous about the questions that might arise on her much-speculated intimacy with Andrei — Inspector Aldo dragged her over the coals many times for his own perverse pleasure during the investigation. She hoped this would not happen today, perhaps a fleeting question might be asked she thought. She detested prying questions as a teenager and was fiercely private, much like Ben.

*   *   *

'Ms Moorecroft, did you believe that Professor Malakov would deliver the ransom money to ensure your safe release?'

'I had no doubt he would, I believed he would arrive, leave the money, and we would drive back to Viareggio.'

Meryl caught the smirk on Inspector Aldo's face as he coughed, drawing her attention, forcing her to look in his direction.

Ben with his familiar old sage nod, encouraged her to go on with her truth.

'You did not believe that he might have been involved in this heist for some sinister reason? That his timeous departure to Russia and your kidnapping seemed to be staged?'

'Not at all sir, I believe, Professor Malakov had no idea this would happen. He was a courteous and chivalrous man in my time with him.'

'Can you please recount the moment of the shooting and the aftermath?'

'I waited for several hours, unsure whether Andrei would call for directions to the place where I was held. The gunshot sent me running in its direction, I was petrified, not knowing if I was going to be shot.'

'Were you not afraid to run towards where you perceived the gunshot had emanated from?'

'I knew instinctively I had to run in that direction. From the distance, I saw Doctor Ben Hart waving, Michael Morrissey was standing over the bleeding Andrei and Inspector Aldo came in behind them, running with a gun poised over his head.'

'Yes, you do know the gunshot was not from Inspector Aldo's gun — evidence has cleared this?'

'Yes sir, I'm aware of this through the inspector.'

'That will be all Ms Moorecroft.'

Court was adjourned until Wednesday leaving them all in the dark as to who will be the next to testify.

*   *   *

Meryl was relieved to find Andrei asleep, the court hearings, suspicions regarding Inspector Aldo and a sense of unease with Gildo Mondo left her in an emotional and mental stupor. Dr.

Spartan declared the surgery a success, the bullet and shrapnel were removed, Andrei's vital signs were steady throughout the procedure. He advised it was best to let Andrei rest overnight. The news that gave her new life was that Andrei would be awake the next day. Doctor Spartan was not sure whether he would remember anything just yet. This was all Meryl needed to hear for now, prior to this situation which had stretched her patience to its limits, she would have pried further for medical information, wanting time-frames and detailed predictions on Andrei's full recovery. She accepted all that was said and was grateful for any small mercy that Andrei would pull through. She hugged a teary-eyed Alec who could not keep his emotions in check as Dr. Spartan addressed them. Ben stood aside when Brad arrived, leaving the two young men to absorb the moment of the news they were waiting for.

While Andrei was not quite out the woods, there was some promising hope.

Chapter 22

Now let it work. Mischief, thou art afoot. Take thou
what course thou wilt."
Shakespeare — Julius Caesar

~

M eryl went on a morning walk to clear her head and relax
before the next court hearing.

She was agitated, fidgety and absent-minded like never before.
Ben watched her with helpless sadness not wanting to unsettle her
further. Meryl knew she had to remain mum on the poison-pen
letter which weighed like a ton of bricks on her already frazzled
state — deception had no place in her relationship with Ben. She
had to centre her energy, to be in the moment with him at breakfast
that morning. She missed talking to Michael but was gradually
coming to terms with their unspoken 'emotional separation'.

As she crossed the Ponte Vecchio a boy accosted her asking
her a question she did not understand, he spoke in Italian in a
dialect that obscured meaning to her foreign ear. She stopped to
ask him to be more specific about what he wanted when he ran
off — she was surrounded by cameras and journalists. Nausea
rose from her belly to her chest, she pushed her way out of the
circle, needing air — footsteps hurried behind her,

'Ms Moorecroft, has Professor Malakov regained consciousness? Do you think his assailant will be discovered soon? How are you coping with the court hearings? What do you think about the judicial system in Italy — no jury — how do you feel about that?'

Meryl realised whether she spoke or not the newspapers and television news would present her as someone who was guilty and running for the hills, she knew she had to say something although her gut reaction was to literally run for hills!

'I cannot comment on the court process and I have no information on Professor Malakov's status,' she blurted out while walking away, in a half running, half walking step. She picked up her pace into a full run, wishing she could slip off her shoes to gain greater speed on the cobbled footpath which threatened to twist her ankles. The footsteps behind her quickened.

Meryl veered down a side lane and got back to the hotel through the service door. She was out of breath and annoyed that her much-needed walk had been rudely interrupted.

'Excuse me, excuse me Ms Moorecroft.'

Hearing this, Meryl rushed to the elevator assuming that reporters had invaded the hotel lobby. She saw the concierge advancing with speed in her direction.

'Are you unwell madam, may I help you up to your room? This can wait till later.'

'I'm ok thank you,' she panted, 'sorry for rushing off, I thought it was... oh never mind, what can wait till later?'

'There's a letter for you madam, I saw you going out earlier, I did not want to send it to your room, I will bring it to you if madam will be so kind as to wait.'

'Yes, of course.'

The letter was in the same durable, ivory coloured envelope as the last letter she received. It was addressed the same way, *Ms Meryl c/o The Eden Hotel*, with a local postage stamp affixed.

Meryl ripped open the envelope before she could shut the door to her room.

Her heart pummelled, leaving her even more breathless after her swift, sprint back to the hotel.

She struggled to clear her head for her next decision.

She reached for the telephone to call Gildo Mondo to set up a meeting as soon as possible. She called Ben to say she would be half an hour late for breakfast. He was happy to wait for her. She had to calm down. She decided a warm bath with a dash of lavender oil would relax her.

Ben was in a cheerful mood and chirped on about a documentary he had watched, he laughed appearing to be very relaxed and jovial.

'It's wonderful to have this leisurely morning with you, darling. I knew you would hold up in your court session. How are you feeling now? It's good to know that Andrei is showing signs of improving, this must be a great relief for you.'

She knew, with guilty regret, that being left for many hours of the day on his own, had contributed to his repetitive comments.

'I was very stressed yesterday at the hearing but am okay now Ben, especially now that we can chat without being too anxious. It is a load off to know that Andrei has a second chance at life although Doctor Spartan is not specific about the recovery. I am now surrendering this to the universe with optimism.'

'Good, that's the best approach to take. Any news from Michael? If you would rather not talk about him, please say so Meryl.'

She knew Ben was still hopeful that she and Michael would somehow get their lives on track.

'It's good that we talk about him Ben, he is happy in South Africa and enjoying the company of his lady friend. I feel we have slipped apart and will need to address that once the time is right,

out of respect for each other. What do you think, 'O wise one?'"
she laughed, trying to remove any indication that she might be
concerned regarding the status of her relationship with Michael.

'I agree, you both should have a face to face discussion if possible and come to a resolution, that is, like you say, respectful
of both your needs. You are, indeed a gracious gal!' he smiled.

'I had to 'mend my ways' as it were, these past weeks putting
'me' on the back burner has been a huge growth point, you know.
I suppose everything happens for a reason. The good thing is
I look at you and I am consoled that my entire world has not
collapsed. *You are as constant as the northern star,* my dear uncle!'
It was good to have this momentary release of tension.

They chatted on for another hour. Ben stayed at the hotel to
finalise his latest article for the medical association and Meryl
had a meeting scheduled with Gildo Mondo.

*   *   *

'To what do I owe the pleasure of your company Ms. Moorecroft?' Gildo Mondo asked with a crinkled frown that added
more folds to his already puffy eyes.

'I don't know where to begin and did not know who to go to.'

'Begin at the beginning is the best way, would you like a glass
of wine?'

'No thanks, Mr. Mondo, I suppose I should start from the
beginning.'

'Gildo, please, drop the formality, may I call you Meryl or if
you prefer, Ms. Meryl?'.

'Meryl will do, thanks,' Meryl felt awkward with this sudden
familiarity from a man who regarded her with some suspicion
in their first meeting.

'I received two, anonymous letters, actually more like notes at the hotel in a space of three days.'

'What sort of letters or notes? Do you have them on you?'

'Yes, I do,' she said pulling them out of her handbag.

'Mmmm. These are threats Ms Meryl, this should be reported to the police as you are involved in an investigation.' Gildo Mondo sat with his eyes closed.

'I am not comfortable with going to Inspector Aldo, sir, this is why I came to you for advice. Consider me your client now.' Meryl was quick to make it clear that she was seeking official, professional, legal advice. She hated being misinterpreted as one wanting to profit from Andrei's situation.

Gildo shot her a narrow-eyed look which made her uneasy again about what he might be thinking.

'Yes, it's good that you have and now that a second note has arrived, it suggests the sender means business.'

He looked at the notes, holding them up close to his puffy eyes and then pulling them back until Meryl felt she had to ask outright what she needed to know.

'Do you think my life is in danger Mr. Mondo?'

'The first note appears nothing to be disturbed about but the second one which does not say much more but includes, *or face what may come.* Now that is what I would be concerned about. No time frame, no reason for what the gripe is and no direct threat of *what may come.*'

'This has everything to do with me being drawn into this case, the first note arrived before my court testimony and the second one after the hearing, this morning. This tells me that someone inside this judicial system has a hand in this, right?'

'My goodness, I can see why you are a writer, Ms Meryl, you might have hit the nail on the head, you know. Do you write crime stories? Although what you say makes complete sense as nobody knows who is being called to the stand in each session.'

'No, no I don't write crime stories,' she said with flustered agitation. 'What do you propose I do as I cannot go to Inspector Aldo with this information?'

'Why is that Ms. Moorecroft?'

He narrowed his eyes again as he studied her face.

She could not determine whether his look was a quizzical or suspicious one.

'I have not told anybody about my suspicions other than Alec Malakov.'

'It's not good to harbour secrets that could potentially jeopardise the judge's decision or your safety.'

'Not damaging to the case but something that I have a hunch about based on my kidnapping.'

'That sounds serious, Ms. Meryl, please proceed, I'm all ears.'

Meryl looked at Gildo Mondo, wondering if placing her trust in him would come back to bite her. She had a momentary unnerving thought, *what if he was in cahoots with Inspector Aldo?* She was in now and had to finish what she started.

'A few days before I was called to the stand, I went unannounced, on a whim, to see Inspector Aldo to ask him when I would be able to start my writing again as he had taken my laptop... ' Meryl broke off as Gildo injected,

'He has your laptop? You are not a suspect in this case Ms Meryl, what reason did he give you for taking your laptop?'

'Nothing much, except that I was not allowed to post anything online with my recently launched weekly blogsite.'

'That is rather a feeble reason, pardon me for saying so, you could use any device to do this? I am beginning to understand why you might be uncomfortable with going to the Inspector. I will order the release of your laptop as soon as possible, now that I am representing you. Mmmm… Andrei detested the inspector for his unorthodox methods. Sorry go on.'

'Well, as I said, I went unannounced to the precinct. Inspector Aldo was in friendly conversation with two men and the voice that riveted me to the spot, was distinctly that of one of the men who took me from the villa. I would know his voice and laugh in my sleep. I heard Aldo say, 'you have nothing to be concerned about, have I ever let you down before?'

'Did Aldo see you?'

'No I hid behind a partitioning wall on the corridor. I caught him off-guard when I called out to him. He appeared uncomfortable for a brief moment.'

'Ms Meryl, this has to be brought before the court, as your abductors at the villa are mooching around this area and the inspector seems to have halted the hunt for them saying that they are not suspects in the shooting. I'm glad you've come forward. As you are a foreigner here, Interpol will have to be informed, leave that to me, we have to ensure your safety Ms Meryl? Is your relative aware of all of this?'

'Ben! Oh no! He would worry and his wellbeing is my concern, Mr Gildo.'

'Yes, the less he knows at this stage and the less others know the better too. Would Alec's partner know about this?'

'I don't know if he does. I am worried as I tend to take a walk very early in the morning and leave the hospital quite late at night.'

'Look, Ms Meryl once I pass this on to Interpol you will have an unobtrusive officer following you, I will ensure you know who he is. Where are you off to now?'

'Thank you, Mr. Mondo that makes me feel better, I'm so glad I came to you. I'm going to the hospital to check in on Andrei.'

'I will come along with you, I want an update on Andrei's recovery too. Ensure that you leave with Alec later this evening, please be alert to your surroundings at all times.'

'Thank you. I hope no media scoundrels are prowling outside the hospital. I should let Ben know that I was bombarded by the media this morning not to shock him when he watches the news tonight.'

'Another thing Ms Meryl, you should be careful with your telephone calls, the media have their ways and means of digging up things by actively listening in.'

Ben's perturbed tone on the other end of the line, his long silence, punctuated by, 'dear, dear, dear' and cautioning words suggested that his jolly disposition that morning was now crushed by his fear of the media hounding her. *What would he say if he knew about the notes she received?*

Circumstances had created a necessary wall between them now.

Chapter 23

Have patience, and endure
Shakespeare — Much Ado about Nothing

~

The conversation with Doctor Spartan had not cleared up any nagging doubts Meryl and Alec had regarding the prognosis for Andrei's full recovery. He said he needed a few more weeks before he could make any conclusive statements. The lingering lines he left them with was shrouded in dubiousness — *I do not want to create false hope, time is essential now, human touch and voice must be felt by him.*

Andrei's eyes were open — the blank, unseeing stare was unsettling. Meryl noticed some colour in his cheeks, his unshaven face was dotted with sprigs of a greying beard — he appeared decades older after the surgery.

'Andrei... its Meryl,' she whispered. His eyes remained fixed, staring straight ahead, acknowledging nothing. She fought back tears as she looked at Alec,

'You should try talking to him Alec, move in a little closer.' Meryl suggested.

'Papa... Andrei, its Alec... come on old sport I need to hear your voice... I miss talking to you. Here press my hand if you hear me.' He looked up at Meryl, his searching eyes wanting some consolation that his father was going to return to the conscious world.

Andrei's eyes lit up for a second, still fixed ahead with a distant, lost look. Alec bent over him and looked into his eyes, 'It's me I'm here in Florence with you, papa!'

Alec, felt a faint, fleeting tightening of his hand.

'Meryl! Meryl! He's tightened his grip, he knows we're here!'

Doctor Spartan walked in.

'Doctor, he responded when I asked him to let me know if he could hear me, he can hear, it's a matter of time before he will speak, right? Alec pleaded.

'Let him rest for a while and return in an hour, he needs baby steps now, one little step at a time, we're not sure what impact too much stimulation might have either.'

Doctor Spartan did not acknowledge anything Alec said. He left them desperate to know more, his evasive, clinical statements made them fearful.

They sat in silence in the coffee shop on the street outside the hospital. Light rain was falling after a beautiful warm day. The rain brought cold air to their night.

'Alec, Doctor Spartan is not giving us much to go on, he could have acknowledged that Andrei was aware you were in the room, talking to him. I would rather know the worst case scenario up front rather than live in hope and then disappointment. First he says Andrei needs human touch and stimulation and then who knows what too much stimulation might do? I am struggling with this, I just need a concrete answer.'

'He must think, I've imagined it, he tightened the grip, it was a slight, gentle pressure, it was fleeting but I know he did, Meryl.'

'I believe you Alec, I saw his eyes light up for a second. I suppose we have to be patient. We have to spend more time with him, if Doctor Spartan allows it.'

'I'm sorry you had no reaction from Andrei, his memory will return, think about the things you said to each other that only you two could have spoken about, say it to him, I'm sure he will remember. I will let you have some time alone with him Meryl, we have to try everything to make him…' Alec could not go on, he paused, 'we're lucky he's alive– yes we have to be patient.'

They sat in prayerful, hopeful, contemplation. Meryl knew that Alec treasured his father's love, it warmed her to feel that good family relationships were possible even though they both came from fractured childhoods.

Her phone cut into her pensive stillness– it was a text message from Michael asking when he could call her.

*   *   *

Michael called at 9 pm.

'Hi Meryl, how are you? I had a text message from Ben saying that Andrei was showing signs of improvement that the surgery went well.'

Meryl was taken aback that Ben did this without consulting her first. He had become fond of Michael during her disappearance when they were thrown together by fate. She caught herself overreacting and stopped herself from saying anything unkind.

'Hi Michael, how are you and… Maci doing…' Meryl was awkward, not sure if she had his lady friend's name correct. She had it fixed in her mind that she was Michael's 'South African lady friend' and neglected to commit her name to memory.

'*Marcia*, she's well Meryl. South Africa is equally lovely as it is terrifying for some who live in fear of crime. Is Andrei going to be ok?'

'He got through the surgery but is not fully aware of where he is or what has happened to him, the doctor did say he was unsure when his memory will return.'

'Have you spoken to him Meryl? About the situation?'

'No Michael, he's not speaking yet. We've been advised that contact has to be in little spurts, not to tire him. The doctor's not committing to too much for fear of a relapse, I think.'

'I'm sorry to hear that, its early days, Meryl, he presented as a determined man from what you told me and what little we know of his life so he has a fighting spirit, I daresay.'

'I hope so Michael.'

'Are you ok, Meryl?'

'Yeah, I am, some good days, some not so good. Being under the scrutiny of the justice system and the media is weighty at times.'

'Are you still being bothered by Inspector Aldo and the media? You should report it, you know Meryl.'

'Yeah, hopefully this will be over soon. I don't want to create any further complications by opening another case against Inspector Aldo or the media. It's exhausting enough, getting through each day hoping nothing new will surface. Tell me a bit about your trip now.'

'I can understand your thinking on that. Well, we have one more place to go to before I head back home. Marcia will stay on for a further two weeks to catch up with friends and family — it's not much of a catch up with me in tow. The people are warm and hospitable — South Africans know how to entertain — its food galore when a guest comes over for a meal. I will have to do more gym days when I get home,' he laughed.

She was happy for him, he sounded relaxed and enjoying the company around him. What he said next is not what she was expecting to hear.

'Meryl, I booked a flight to Florence, to see you for few days before I get back home, Greg has been gracious about this brief extension on my leave.'

'You've booked already? When do you arrive?' Once those words escaped her, she wondered whether she sounded like his visit was an invasion.

'I hope it won't be inconvenient or is my timing bad? I will be staying at the Hotel Eden too.'

'Oh, no, not inconvenient, I'm a little surprised, I did not expect you to be back in Florence this soon, what with the trip to South Africa. I know how you are with work, remember? Ben will be glad to see you Michael. It's not inconvenient, it's just that the trial is in session and I might be out some days and I spend quite a few hours each evening at the hospital.'

She knew she had to stop talking.

Michael felt the strain in Meryl's voice, he felt something was afoot. He knew he did not have the right to pry anymore.

'That's okay Meryl, as long as I see that you're fine that's all that matters. I know you are under tremendous pressure, I promise I'll be there for just six days. I will not get in the way.'

She felt the old Michael in those lines, begging to be allowed, resisting her cautious undertones.

'It will be good to see you Michael. You won't be disturbing me at all. Take care now and keep me posted on the day and time you arrive. Enjoy the next leg, or the final leg of your South African experience. I look forward to hearing more about it when you get here.'

'Bye Meryl, chat again soon.'

Michael felt like years had passed since Meryl's departure. She made her choices and life had thrown her a curve ball. He had not expected to be in South Africa, without her, but his life-path veered on a different journey.

She lay in bed contemplating whether she should call Ben. The clock at her bedside glowed at 11:00 pm. It was too late to call now.

*   *   *

The rain had not cleared, it was a wet morning. Meryl and Ben ordered room service breakfast. She went over to Ben's room.

'What time did you get in from the hospital? I read until 11 pm and thought you might stop over for a chat on your return.'

I got in at about 9 pm, Michael called. I thought it was too late to call you, I should have sent you a text message, I think too much is going on in my little head these days.'

'Is everything ok with Andrei?'

'Yes not much change except that he is conscious but not talking.'

'That's a positive sign, you will need to spend more time with him now to coax him into a rapid recovery? Everything okay with Michael? I sent him a message about Andrei's surgery, I hope you don't mind, Meryl.'

'Not at all,' she fibbed, 'it was good to chat with him. Did he tell you he's coming to Florence soon?'

'No. When will he be here?' Meryl fought back thinking that Ben sounded pleased that Michael was returning to Florence.

'He will send through the details soon. He's enjoying South Africa. I think he would love to live there if the opportunity presented itself.'

'Really? I thought he enjoyed what he did.'

'Yes he does, I think, he would enjoy doing the same role in South Africa.'

'Interesting. Eat up now, cold scrambled eggs — not my cup

of tea! I ordered French toast for you, I know you eat like a bird before these court hearings.'

Neither of them had anticipated that Boris would be called to the stand that day.

Chapter 24

Thou liest, thou thread, thou thimble, thou yard,
three-quarters, half-yeard, quarter, nail! Thou flea,
thou nit, thou winter cricket thou!
Shakespeare — The Taming of the Shrew

~

B oris Malakov, thirty-eight years old, strode towards the
prosecutor with the ease of a man without a care nor concern in the world.

Meryl looked at him, searching for any resemblance to Andrei.

Not a trace.

Alec smiled Andrei's smile with the early signs of lines encircling his eyes. Alec, too, had bright, dark curious, child-like eyes.

'Cite your full name.'

'Boris Aleksandra Malakov.'

Meryl remembered that deep voice from her days of incarceration where sounds became significant in her cave of darkness. She shivered as she recalled how quickly he switched from sounding gentle to being angry and threatening.

Ben and Brad were in court this morning to support Alec in anticipation of the bombshells Boris might drop.

The prosecutor continued with his questions with unwavering eyes on Boris Malakov.

'What was the nature of your business in Florence, during this trip?'

'I had business matters to attend to.'

'Can you please specify the nature of your business?'

'I am CEO of the shoe factory in Russia. I was here on a mission to find more retail outlets that wanted to stock and sell our leather shoes.'

'Did you have people working here for you or assisting you?'

'Yes, I have connections with a few locals so they help when I need them.'

'How many people do you engage to assist you? Please name them?'

'Three men, Mikhail Sabella, Leo Benedetti and Francois Dupain.'

'Where were you on the day Professor Andrei Malakov was shot?'

'I was here in Florence at my apartment.'

'Where were you the day before he was shot?'

'I made a trip to Pelago.'

'What was the nature of your business there?'

'I went to see Gildo Mondo, Andrei's lawyer.'

The hush in court and a faint gasp from a few, forced the judge to look up long and hard at Boris Malakov before he glanced with curiosity at Gildo Mondo in the public gallery.

Meryl hung onto Ben's arm, waiting for what would follow.

'What was the reason for this visit?'

'I needed to find out if he knew what Andrei was doing in Florence before he arrived in Moscow, the week before he was shot.'

'Please answer just 'yes' or 'no' to my next question. Is it fair to assume you and Professor Malakov were not on favourable terms?'

'Yes.' Boris said without flinching, without a care, staring at the wall behind the judge.

'Were you in the villa on the night of Ms Moorecroft's abduction?'

'No.'

'Where were you on the night in question?'

'At my apartment.'

'Did you order the men at the villa to kidnap Ms Moorecroft?'

'No, I did not know she was at the villa.'

'Remember you are under oath Mr Malakov.'

'I am telling you the truth and you don't believe me?

'Did you know she was with Professor Malakov at the villa?'

'That I knew from the time she arrived there. I told Dmitri to have her removed before the men went out to the villa that night. I did not know she was still there.'

'You ordered the ransacking of the villa and when Ms Moorecroft's presence was discovered, you ordered the kidnapping.'

'I did not know she was there, I said. How many more times am I expected to say this?'

'Ms Moorecroft has testified that the men downstairs in the professor's study called someone, we have evidence that they called you.'

'Yes, they called me but it was not about Ms Moorecroft. They could not find the manuscript I sent them to look for.'

'Explain to the judge why you needed this manuscript you refer to.'

'Professor Malakov, my stepfather as you all know, was trying to destroy the shoe empire my grandfather spent his lifetime creating. He was writing an article for *Time* magazine to expose my grandfather on some unfounded belief he had and I believe he was writing a book too on my mother's family.'

'Did you speak to Professor Malakov about being unhappy with this exposé?'

'You kidding me! He is a very unapproachable man at the best of times.'

Meryl and Alec flinched in their seats at the description of Andrei as a man they both knew to be different to such an evaluation of his personality. Meryl had overheard Andrei's flustered telephone conversation in his study in Viareggio but nothing about him was 'unapproachable.'

The prosecutor continued.

'So without asking the professor, you went ahead and ransacked his premises and carried out the kidnapping of Ms. Moorecroft?'

'Yes to the first part and, no to the second part.'

'Explain why you say 'no' to the second part, as you do.'

'The men, Mikhail, Leo and Francoise were to take the papers only. I only realised they had the lady, Ms Moorecroft, when they called me from the vehicle, that is the second call they made, if you check your records for that night, saying that the woman was in the upstairs bedroom trying to call someone so they had to take her to allow them a safe getaway.'

'Mr Malakov, help us understand how you expect us to believe that you had nothing to do with the abduction of Ms. Moorecroft, no intent, when a ransom of twenty-five million US dollars was asked for? The court is aware that your shoe business is in financial dire straits, almost going into receivership. We have proof of this.'

'Yes that is well and good, you did your homework, but your sums are wrong! I did not ask for the money, I wanted the manuscripts for the magazine and apparent book.' Boris was out of line as he yelled at the prosecutor. The judge fidgeted with his papers as he called a short break of fifteen minutes.

*   *   *

Alec was tired and morose. Brad stood by silent. Meryl and Ben had to break the ice. Meryl began,

'Thankfully the judge called for a short break. I was worried Boris would lunge at the prosecutor, he has a volatile temper.'

'Yes,' agreed Brad.

'I was expecting fireworks from Boris, to be honest, that's the way he always deals with being held accountable,' Alec said.

Ben became aware that they were being watched, 'don't make it too obvious, there's a man watching us, trying to be furtive from across the courtyard, he is definitely watching us. He's does not appear to be a reporter, I wonder what he's up to?'

Brad looked up and noticed the man, he looked down at the ground and whispered, 'I see him, you are right.'

Alec tried to calm Ben, 'Ben, he appears to be looking our way, it must be a curious person who is following the case and has figured out we are in some way connected to it, I don't think it's anything to be perturbed about.'

Meryl could have hugged Alec for his consideration of Ben when he was going through turbulent emotions himself.

'You could be right, I think Alec. My imagination is getting the better of me,' Ben laughed.

*   *   *

The court was back in session. A red-faced Boris was in his seat, no doubt having had a telling off from the judge behind closed doors.

'Mr Malakov, you have to explain the ransom that Ms Moorecroft had to ask the professor for on instruction from you.'

'Francois Dupain is in some trouble and needed the money, he added the ransom request; it was not my doing. He was trying to make something on the side, I did not stop him, so that makes *me* guilty, right?'

'Something *big* on the side is more like it Mr Malakov. So you were aware of his plans and yes it makes you complicit if you did not think to stop him.'

'I had him do as I asked, anything extra was his own doing, unrelated to me.'

'Where is Francois Dupain, Mikhail Sabella and Leo Benedetti at this time?'

'I don't know sir.'

'You've had no contact with them since your father was shot?'

'No, and he is my stepfather, let's keep that clear.'

Meryl heard Ben mouth under his breath, 'dear, dear, dear what an insolent lad.'

She smiled and moved a little closer to him.

'Our investigation shows that you spoke to Mikhail Sabella fifteen minutes before Andrei Malakov was shot and the mobile tower location indicated you were in the vicinity about two kilometres away from where the shooting took place. This would have given you time to get away after you shot your father.'

'Yes, I did call him as I heard the gunshots. I did not shoot Andrei Malakov.'

'Once we have the men in custody, we will know the truth Mr Malakov. One further question is, how did you know that the professor was writing a book and articles on the shoe business in Moscow?'

'Ana and Dmitri kept me informed, more Ana than Dmitri. She loves me and has my best interests at heart unlike Andrei Malakov.'

Alec was relieved when the judge declared the session closed for that day to resume the following morning at 11 am. He had heard more than he could endure for the day.

*   *   *

Meryl was asked to meet with the Inspector from Interpol which was arranged by Gildo Mondo for her to identify two men they suspected were Mikhail Sabella and Leo Benedetti, Boris' partners in crime.

Meryl had to listen in to voice recordings of both men as that was her only means of identifying them. Voices was all she heard en-route to the prison she was kept in.

She confirmed both men were her kidnappers.

The Frenchman, Francoise Dupain was missing.

Nobody knew where he was.

Meryl was relieved that two were now in custody and knew they would be the next two to be questioned. She hoped this meant the end to the notes she had received.

Brad, Meryl and Alec went out for a quiet drink after the hectic proceedings of the day. Ben retired for the day.

'Gee, that was a close call with the plain clothes police officer watching us. Poor Ben, I feel awful having to lie to him.' Meryl bemoaned.

'Its best he is oblivious to the media harassment you've been facing and if he knows about the notes you received, who knows how he'll react.' Alec was concerned that Ben should be protected.

Brad intervened, 'Meryl, you will have to tell him at some point, you both are very close and you share a loving relationship. I would be saddened if withholding this, tests your relationship once he finds out. Won't he be assured that you are safe now that you are being safely followed and protected?'

'Yes, I know, I will have to tell him and your reasoning makes sense Brad, thank you.'

Alec looked at Brad, 'I don't think Meryl's and Ben's relationship will ever be tested, understanding will prevail once he knows. Meryl has to wait for the appropriate time to tell him. Today is out of the question, his nerves have been stretched just as ours have been.'

They debriefed the court proceedings of the day. Alec confirmed again that Boris' reactions were pretty much like the Boris he knew, nothing out of the ordinary.

Brad commented on Ana's involvement with Boris after all that Andrei had done to give her a new life. They finally agreed that Boris was the only family Ana had and she felt an obligation to do his bidding even if it got her a prison sentence.

Meryl knew that she would be writing many blogposts after the case on dangerous allegiances. She was promised by Gildo Mondo that her laptop would be returned once Interpol spoke to Inspector Aldo.

She pondered upon Inspector Aldo's aloofness of late, he kept his distance during Boris' hearing. He did not seek her out in the fifteen-minute court break to throw around his customary acerbic judgements of Andrei's character.

'Odd, very odd indeed,' she thought.

Chapter 25

My bounty is as boundless as the sea,
My love as deep; the more I give to thee
The more I have, for both are infinite
Shakespeare — Romeo and Juliet

~

The journey to Pietermaritzburg, the inland town from the coastal city of Durban was a short drive. Marcia was excited, the city brought back fond memories of holidays spent at Mama Dolores' sister's home with her cousins. Mama Thembu was like a second mother to Marcia, she taught her much about culture and traditions. Dolores had become a little westernised — all those years of voracious reading had given her a different head, a different view on life. Marcia was grateful for her rich upbringing and was very eager to share this with Michael.

They booked into a bed and breakfast guest house, Marcia hired a car for their drive to Mama Thembu who lived on the outskirts of the city. The week they were to spend in Pietermaritzburg was packed with activities; from visiting old college friends, family and, two days at the Drakensburg Mountains, to a day out on the Midlands meander route to take in all the sights and cottage industries along the way. Michael enjoyed having plans made for him, this is what he was comfortable with. His mother and sister arranged his life before he met Meryl. Now Marcia assumed a similar role on this tour. He enjoyed taking the backseat on this trip.

Mama Thembu's home, nestled in mountainous terrain on dusty winding roads, after a bumpy ride, came as a surprise to Michael.

Young men and women dressed in traditional costume and elders dressed in their church uniforms welcomed Michael and Marcia — the singing and vibrant ululating could be heard as they stepped out the vehicle which was a distance away, on their upward, on foot, trek to the little house on the hill. They were surrounded by the dancing, singing troupe, all of whom were Marcia's relatives. It was akin to a royal reception. Michael heard the words, '*Welcome, welcome, Michael*' intermingled with melodious indigenous singing. He loved the way his name was pronounced, *My-kale* — such unrestricted outpouring of love left Michael speechless, overwhelmed by it all. In a sudden rush, Marcia was lifted up and carried to the house where Mama Thembu sat, looking serene, in a motorised wheelchair.

This was an emotional moment for Marcia who was seeing Mama Thembu for the first time, outdoors, in a wheelchair. She became paralysed several years ago after an illness which was misdiagnosed through poor medical management under Bantu Affairs. She had spent many years in bed, in a chair, barely leaving home. The wheelchair was Marcia's gift to her while she was away working overseas. Mama Thembu was mobile, smiling and glowing with joy as she hugged Marcia which left Michael emotional too, he was infused by the authentic, raw expression of love and gratitude. He grew up with keeping one's emotions in check, here emotional expressions whether joy or sadness was expressed without restraint.

Michael sat on the ground with Marcia at the feet of Mama Thembu in traditional respect given to the elder and mother of the home.

'Welcome Michael, we are so happy to have you here in our home. I hope you are enjoying your visit to South Africa.' Mama Thembu's voice was rich, deep, melodious and warm. Her eyes told the experience of one who had seen dark days of suffering through to the transition to modern day South Africa. She held a wizened, prophetess air about her that was quite magnetic. Her wide smile glowed from the depths of her soul.

'Thank you, thank you,' was all Michael could say as she held both his hands in hers.

'When Marcia said she was bringing a friend, we were so happy to know she has such a good friend in you. We are so pleased that you came all the way here to meet us. Marcia is an angel, our angel, she always puts her family first. Its time she started looking after herself now. I can enjoy the outdoors again, thanks to my angel. I know you don't want me to praise you, Marcia, you are lucky too, blessed Michael, to have Marcia as your friend, I'm not sure if you are her boyfriend, I'm waiting to hear from her on that. She is a bit secretive about these things, you know,' she laughed.

'I am lucky and blessed to have met your angel, I am very happy to be here Mama,' he said. Marcia was moved by the humble respect he showed Mama Thembu.

Michael knew it was best not to say anything to Marcia's family – he loved her from the depths of his being – he hoped she realised how much he wanted to spend the rest of his life with her – he wanted to be part of her family whose love was boundless.

A royal feast of traditional food and roast meats were served, the women, strong women, young and old, held this family up, woven together like a colourful, protective blanket. Michael allowed himself to bask in the unbridled show of warmth and acceptance of his presence.

He knew it was time to talk to Marcia about their 'relationship' before he left for Florence.

* * *

That night back at the hotel, still in separate rooms, Michael asked Marcia to join him for drinks.

She was dressed in a brightly coloured blue and green Swazi kaftan and large, dangling, wooden earrings which Mama Thembu had given her with a whispered, 'never forget who you are and where you come from, angel.'

She looked relaxed and happy.

'Hey, Michael, what's up with the late-night rendezvous, it must be urgent if it couldn't wait until morning, is something the matter?'

'I'm not sure if I will call it urgent as much as that my heart yearns to know...'

Marcia felt the blood rise to her face, her heart quickened, she knew how she felt, she knew she was denying what could never be hers in reality... she knew Michael was heading to Florence soon...

'This sounds serious, what is it?'

'I know you have avoided any intimacy since I returned from Italy and insisted on booking separate rooms on this trip... tell me Marcia, do you feel anything for me? I love you with all my heart... There, I've said it and I need to know whether I have a chance with you, not just as a friend, but as my lifetime partner, as my future wife?' His voice was low, hoarse, breaking with emotional weight, he looked vulnerable in this moment as he poured his heart to her.

Marcia, looked at him, her eyes threatened to well up with the tears she had withheld for some time, only shedding them in private moments. She remained silent for a long time. Her mind buzzed, how did this happen, did she deserve this and what happens to Meryl now? She had to let him know exactly how she felt, this friendship was too special to be sullied by passionate pleas or romanticised notions that might have emerged under the cultural seduction of a new world. She had to remain true to herself and yet... yet here in front of her was a man she had already given her heart to, he did not know it, he was waiting to hear it, she had to be true to herself...

'Michael, dearest Michael, what a situation we find ourselves in. I gave you my heart some time ago, truth be told, but I'm all too aware that you have much going on in your private world. Meryl cannot be obliterated, from my mind anyway. If you were a free man, I would say yes in a heartbeat, I don't know why I should deserve a man like you. I'm afraid that this fairytale will end. I am so afraid my heart will be broken and this fear makes me believe that I don't deserve this, from... a man like you...' she broke off as she looked away, not knowing what else to say. She cringed, hoping that she did not come across as a complete and utter fool.

'Marcia, it makes my heart soar with joy that you feel the same way. I understand your reservation, I really do, we did not start on a perfect platform, for want of a better word, but my trip to Florence next week is with a purpose. I have been looking for the appropriate moment to say this to you. I am ending it with Meryl, we both know it has already ended but we do owe each other a face to face, respectful severing. I know I will have to be there for Meryl as moral support from time to time with the trial and Andrei's recovery. She does not appear to need my moral support but I will be there, to be honest, should she need to sound the situation out with me as a neutral ally. I don't know how you feel about this.'

'I would not expect any less of you Michael, this is the man I've come to know and love. How can I expect you to cast her aside when she needs a friend like you, now at this crucial time in her life? I have to be honest to myself too, I need to know whether you are ending this with Meryl because of how you feel for me.'

'That would be the primary reason if I am true to myself, however, we were drifting apart for almost a year before she set out on her sabbatical in search of new meaning in her life. I knew the gap widened after she met the professor, I have accepted that she has moved on. She too, has to say it to me, we both have to be upfront with each other. I want her to be happy without the current stress she is under.'

'I appreciate your honesty, Michael. Let's leave things as they are until you go to Florence and sort out what you need to. I will be waiting for you, if you still feel the same way when you return.'

'Marcia, you scare me with your rational, unemotional stance now. I love you from the core of my being. I want to be with you until the end of my days, I want to be the father of your children, I want you and need you in my life and I need you to know that my heart is not fickle. If it makes you happy to wait, I will honour that, even though I want to be engaged to you before I head back home to wait for your return. If I am rushing you, going too fast, please stop me. I have held this inside me for too long.'

'I don't mean to sound rational and unemotional, far from it, it might be my female family strength coming across I suppose, Mama D and Mama T have left this mark on me you know, it's that *pick yourself up, look up at the stars, keep your dignity intact* attitude. It's my way of protecting my heart,' she smiled.

She walked across to Michael and kissed him with ardent hope and desire. This raw honesty and integrity is what stole her heart all those months ago. She nestled her head against his big, beautiful, beating heart.

'I will be waiting for your return from Florence to start our new life together.' She said this, while looking directly at him. She no longer looked away with her head bowed. She was no longer afraid to be acknowledged and loved.

He held her close against him, his emotion-laden whisper, 'stay with me tonight, my love, now and always, please Marcia,' is all she needed to hear.

Chapter 26

Are you sure/That we are awake? It seems to me/
That yet we sleep, we dream
Shakespeare — A Midsummer Night's Dream

~

A ndrei's speech returned.
Meryl's and Alec's hope was reignited in the shared world
that connected them to Andrei, their warm friendship grew
stronger each day.

Dr Spartan gave the green light for Andrei to hold a video
testimony of the day he was shot. In trickling bits at first, his
memory resurfaced from the fog of the past months. Alec
recorded each lucid memory as it emerged.

Meryl's step was lighter, she glowed with warm gratitude.

She heard once again, after three long months of waiting,
the magical way in which Andrei said *'Merryl'* with a lilting
slow drawl of the 'r' that never ceased to delight her. That he
remembered her and was happy *she* was safe made the waiting,
the angst, and the challenges worthwhile. That he was alive
and well was all she could have hoped for. He had many hours
of physical therapy ahead of him to strengthen his limbs and
to re-learn how to use them again.

*　　*　　*

Andrei's video conference, recounting the day he was shot and the days prior, was set up in his hospital private room with the prosecutor and the judge hooked up from the court chambers.

Nobody, apart from police officials were allowed to sit in with Andrei, Meryl and Alec were granted permission to sit out in the hallway should he need any emotional support. Two nurses and the doctor were on standby too. Two police inspectors, one from Florence, the other an Interpol inspector were in the room with Andrei. The IT tech team were on standby out in the hallway once the session was in progress.

Andrei was shaved, his hair combed back to reveal a bony, angular face with large hollowed eyes; he spoke very slowly, stopping to relax as he proceeded to answer each question. The session went on for forty minutes.

The prosecutor shed his stiff attitude.

'Professor Malakov, indicate if you can see and hear us clearly,' the prosecutor said.

'Andrei smiled saying, 'yes sir, I see you both.'

'Can you please tell us what happened after Ms. Moorecroft called you regarding her abduction and the ransom demand? Take your time, we do not have to complete this all at once today. Just your recollections of the events, please, Professor Malakov.'

'Thank you, yes, I got the abrupt call and could not get in touch with Ms Moorecroft thereafter, the line was disconnected. A man with a French accent called me, he told me where to drive to. I was told to place the money in a black SUV which would be parked near the river. Once the money was placed in the boot of the vehicle, I was told that Ms Moorecroft would call me with directions on how to get to her.'

Andrei shut his eyes for a few seconds.

'That's good, Professor Malakov, are you able to go on or would you like a short break?' the judge intervened.

'Two minutes, I need a drink of water and I will continue.'

The nurse was summoned to assist Andrei as he slowly sipped some water through a straw. He had partial paralysis on the left side of his face which made pursing his lips to sip the water impossible, all he could do was suck in a little water with great effort.

'I am ready to go on now,' he said.

'Thank you Professor Malakov, narrate the details as you remember from that point on.'

'I placed the money in the boot of the SUV, as I turned around to wait for *Merryl's*, Ms Moorecroft's call, a gunshot was fired from the bushland to the left of my vehicle. Instinct made me run, I had no idea which direction to go in so I ran hoping that I would find Ms Moorecroft along the way or that she would call to tell me where she was.'

'I see, that's good, your memory is quite distinct. When was the second shot fired, the one that hit you?'

Andrei paused for a few minutes, closed his eyes as though reliving the moment before he said,

'I kept running until I saw the road to the right of me through the clearing, I ran through the clearing wanting to get onto the road when I heard footsteps advancing behind me, crackling on the dry fallen leaves and branches. I reached the road and continued running, I turned around to see who was approaching when the second shot was fired. As the bullet hit me, I saw a tall, lean figure that appeared to be a man, darting out of view. That is all I remember, I must have passed out, I think.'

'If you are up to it and not too tired, can you remember any details of the man you saw dart out of view? Did he have a gun? Was he familiar?'

'I can recall, that he had a gun in his hand which was lowered to his side as I went down, I'm afraid that's all I remember for now.'

'One last question, did you notice any other movement, or signs that other people were around?'

'No, I did not hear anything else nor see anyone else — when I heard the footsteps behind me, I turned because I thought I heard the sound of a car approaching, but nothing was visible — the place was very still, isolated.'

'Thank you Professor Malakov, you should rest now. Please do not enter into a discussion on this with your son and Ms Moorecroft.'

'Certainly, I understand, thank you for your patience.'

'If you remember anything, please tell Doctor Spartan to call me. If we need to speak to you again, it will be with your doctor's approval. Rest well Professor Malakov.'

Andrei shut his eyes and fell asleep for several hours.

*   *   *

He was running, he was out of breath, he had to get to Meryl, the gunshot made him anxious for her safety. Was she alive, was she injured? He felt so responsible for all that had happened, he should not have left her alone at the villa. How could he have put her in harm's way? The footsteps in the bushland behind him seemed to grow closer, swifter. He heard a vehicle approaching, it sounded like a small car, he could not pick up how close it was. Could it be Meryl? He turned around, the second shot hit him, he looked across into the thicket — a man was lowering his arm, in his hand was a gun... he knew the man, this thin, tall man who darted out of view. He tried to shout out as his voice echoed in his head, everything around him became hazy, his legs buckled as he hit the surface of the road...

*　　*　　*

The video conference was strenuous for Andrei, it was the longest he sustained attention and communication since the surgery. Brad was leaving for New York later that day to attend to urgent work matters. Alec and Meryl met Ben and Brad for lunch to debrief the proceedings of the last day.

'I hope Andrei was not too exhausted from his video conference with the courts, he's doing well with his recovery and should not be distressed in any way.' Ben showed his consternation with sincerity as one who cared on a personal level and as a medical man himself. 'What did Doctor Spartan say after the session?'

'We were advised not to disturb Andrei. Reliving the harrowing experience and recalling with clarity and accuracy the events of that day exhausted him.' Meryl was concerned that Andrei was considerably weaker after this.

'We must see this to its closure. I will only rest once Andrei is back home with me, you know,' Alec looked at Meryl as he said this, aware that she would want to be around Andrei through to his full recovery.

'Yes, he must want that too Alec,' she said with a quiet, softer voice, trying to conceal her surging emotions. 'We want the best for him.'

*　　*　　*

Andrei was wide awake and waiting for Meryl and Alec to arrive the following evening.

'How are you doing, Andrei? We were under instruction to let you rest, so here we are and so happy to be with you.' Meryl said this with the tenderness and care of old love.

'I'm ok *moya zvezda*, just a little headache this evening, how are you and Alec holding up?' Andrei looked at Alec with loving concern.

As much as she wanted every waking moment with Andrei now that he was able to hear them and speak to them, she left father and son to have some private time. Andrei's eyes followed her as she walked out. She was at the door where she lingered when she overheard Andrei,

'You ok, *darling*? I am worried about you, I'm so glad, *Merryl* is here for you. She is a very special lady, she was destined to come to me and into our lives, nothing happens without a reason Alec.'

Meryl hurried away as her overwrought emotions gave way, gushing into a rivulet of tears, such tenderness for his grown son spoke volumes of the capacity of this man to love unconditionally. To speak of her so fondly too, in his time of need confirmed his selflessness. Whatever life was going to serve her from here on, she knew she would always be grateful for the *chair borrower, roving professor with a smile that encircled his bright curious eyes* that fateful day they met, many months ago in Bath, a place she loved returning to where many memories were made. She had much more to learn about his experience in Russia, she had second-hand accounts of Ana and Dmitri, two unreliable bearers of Andrei's truth. Andrei trusted them with his life and here he was now — the two people he saved from injustice were in part responsible for his attack that almost claimed his life. She knew he had a long way to go with his recovery, intensive physiotherapy and perhaps more surgery depending on how soon he would recover full movement of his spine and limbs.

It was a warm evening. She looked up at the star-filled sky, she was his brightest star, his *zvezda* not so long ago, before, that dreadful day he was shot. Would they regain the bond that had started to grow like a steady light between them?

A thousand questions hung with the hopeful weight of a million bright stars, filling her with restless yearning.

What would the months ahead bring?

In time vindication might be possible.

Chapter 27

This above all; to thine own self be true.
(Shakespeare — Hamlet)

~

Andrei's progress brought good days and days when hope was tested with the passage of time. Many hours in physical therapy was beginning to frustrate him. Arms, legs and neck coordination needed intense work. Mariya, who did not take Andrei's last name, passed away peacefully in her home in Moscow. Alec left to attend the funeral, with Andrei's blessings, to pay his last respects to his mother.

Boris was not allowed to leave the country.

*   *   *

Mikhail Sabella and Leo Benedetti were taken into custody after Meryl confirmed they were her abductors. Francoise Dupain was still a mystery. Questions, whether he had skipped the country surfaced. He did not appear to have had a falling out with Boris. The question the media speculated and bandied about was, *where was the money?* Not much attention was given to who actually shot Andrei.

Gildo Mondo had the laptop that Inspector Aldo unofficially confiscated from Meryl. She decided to take a walk over to meet him and reclaim her prized possession.

Her unobtrusive protector followed some distance behind her. As she passed the bakery two blocks from her hotel, two people, a cameraman and a journalist jumped out of the alleyway, scaring her, rooting her to the spot, bombarding her with,

'Ms Moorecroft, are you staying on in Italy, the case is almost over now, what's your plans? You know you are known as the *zvezda of Viareggio and olive girl*, right? Where to from here?'

The plain clothes police officer rushed in between Meryl and the voracious journalist who hungered after a juicy bit of sensationalism.

'I will have you all arrested for harassment, enough now!'

'We are working, what's wrong with that?' snapped the young journalist.

Meryl was instructed to quicken her walking pace, the officer hailed a cab and got her safely to Gildo Mondo's hotel.

She was relieved to see her laptop on the seat beside him.

'What's wrong, Ms. Moorecroft, you are as white as a sheet, are you unwell?' he asked.

'No, no, I was bombarded by the media again as I left my hotel, I should be used to this now, I suppose, it's such an invasion of privacy, you know. I'm beginning to think it might not be such a good idea to post anymore blogs if this is going to go on while I'm here.'

'Nonsense! I've cleared it with the judge, you do as you please, the case is about to close, hold off for a day or two before posting any of your thoughts on the case, is my recommendation but it's up to you, Ms Meryl. The judge's verdict will be issued in two days anyway.'

'Thank you, I will hold off to be safe from any further media onslaughts and poison-pen letters! I cannot thank you enough for all you have done to help me Mr. Mondo.' She felt the urge to hug Gildo Mondo and stopped herself in the nick of time — her enthusiasm might be misinterpreted, she thought.

'Gildo, please, Andrei would not have it any other way you know,' he smiled.

*   *   *

Michael arrived in Florence the afternoon before the final sentence hearings. Meryl noted his buoyant spirit, he appeared younger, calmer and more relaxed — the trip to South Africa seemed to have energised him with a spirit that Meryl enjoyed seeing.

They met Ben for dinner that night. Seeing Michael was like seeing an old friend or long-lost family member again and not the lover she shared so many significant years with. Ben retired, tactfully early for the night, saying he needed his beauty sleep before the big day of sentencing that required him to be fully alert.

'Ben, still as thoughtful as ever in giving us some 'alone' time,' Michael observed.

'He has been my rock through these months here, you don't know the half of what's been going on. It will be over soon thankfully. God willing, that is.'

'I'm sorry to hear that Meryl, I wish you kept me in the loop. Are you able to hang on for much longer?'

Michael felt guilty, he realised he had to choose the day and his words carefully not to wound Meryl. He observed how tired she looked, dark shadows under her eyes, and lines that had deepened on her forehead since he last saw her, made him uneasy. Her customary attention to detail in her dress sense had declined, she wore a pair of creased jeans and a light crumpled cardigan. What he had come to settle, had to wait.

'I didn't want to pour my troubles on you Michael, you were on a great trip in South Africa and the last thing you needed was me calling you with my *damsel in distress* matters. I knew it would disturb you and ruin your holiday. How is Marcia doing, is she still in South Africa?'

'Not at all Meryl, it's good to talk to a neutral ear sometimes. Marcia's well, I realised how much of her life is still there in South Africa. She will stay on for another two weeks before she has to return to work. I'll see her then, when we are both back home.'

Meryl listened, knowing that Michael had given his heart to Marcia, the look in his eyes said it all when he spoke of her. She felt happy for him, no tantrums from her anymore. She wanted him to be happy, he was a good man and deserved a life where he was valued not only for his work but for the man he was too. She knew letting him go would create a void in her life that she had to accept, this was a choice she made which was a difficult situation for him to accept at first. She appreciated that he stepped aside after the initial resistance to allow her the time and space she craved.

She filled him in on all that had transpired during the past three months. After she had said all she wanted to say on the court hearings and Andrei's condition, she looked at him with a soft, gentle smile.

What she said left him speechless, she knew him so well, so often she said what he was thinking or she would call him on a matter that was on his mind in that particular moment. He often wondered if it was being close to someone that created this psychic energy or was it just a special quality that some had. He knew he lacked that quality, he had put his foot into things many times over the years.

'Michael, we have drifted apart, we would be foolish to think otherwise, I know I cannot be that person I was ten years ago. I know, you need to be with someone who is present in the moment with you, I'm off with my thoughts, enjoying my seclusion and wafting from day to day. You are a practical person, we shared many, many wonderful years which I will always cherish. I could never expect you to be waiting for something that won't happen and miss the golden opportunity that life is throwing at you right now. If I am true to myself, I will say to you now,' she reached across the table, taking both his hands in hers, 'we respect each other too much, not to set each other free; we shall always share a warm friendship. Time has brought us life lessons, time must be grabbed now to make the most of what we both have found. Don't regret nor be sad, Michael. I believe, I won't say, I know, I believe, you are in a beautiful phase of your life, don't let Marcia slip away.' Her eyes could not conceal the emotions behind her words. This was the most difficult thing she had to do in her life. She fought back the tears as she held onto her conviction, to speak her truth without hurting the beautiful soul before her.

Michael looked at her, his eyes red, his voice heavy, all he was able to say was,

'Thank you Meryl, thank you.'

He clasped her hands, reaching over as he pulled her hands up to his chest, in quiet acknowledgement that this was as it should be if they were to be happy.

All else around them did not exist as they absorbed the decision they both had to accept if they were to allow each other to grow in their own sunlight.

No explanations, no bitterness. Time could never erase what they once had.

* * *

She sat in the glow of the white light of her laptop, with a slow, light and steady tap on the keyboard, she started a new page, a new blog.

Letting Go
Nothing in life is permanent.

Attachments create pain and grief. Knowing when to say what is true to the essence of one's being is essential when either discovering new love or when acknowledging that some relationships no longer fit. It is not so much the letting go as 'how to let go.' Anger and animosity have no place in the gentle releasing, the letting go, that fear of loss prevents. Anger and animosity cannot enshrine what was once a wonderful, shared life. Memories don't die, they become shelved in the recesses of one's mind, resurfacing when the triggers of life reignite them, lighting up the heart, in a warm glow of remembrance. Regret has no place in the joys and love once shared.

Memory is permanent and life's encounters, transient.
Parting is such sweet sorrow.

She felt a quiet peace surround her as she shut down her laptop.

Chapter 28

Life's but a walking shadow, a poor player
That struts and frets his hour upon the stage,
And then is heard no more. It is a tale
Told by an idiot, full of sound and fury,
Signifying nothing.
Shakespeare — Macbeth

~

Much had come to light before the final verdict was announced.

Inspector Aldo who had made himself scarce in recent weeks was the subject under extensive scrutiny. The two bullets expelled on the night of Andrei's shooting were emitted from different guns, one was from an FN Browning, semi-automatic pistol. The bullets found in a gun dredged from the river close to where Andrei was shot, was a Heckler & Koch MP5SF, a private firearm purchased by Inspector Aldo three months before from a UK gun dealer. The calibre of bullet lodged in Andrei's skull matched those still in the chamber of the gun that was tossed into the river. A black leather holster was also salvaged from the river — further investigation revealed that

Inspector Aldo bought the holster on the same day the gun was purchased.

After many days of focusing on the figure that Andrei saw on the day he was shot, he confirmed that the male figure in the scrub fitted that of Inspector Aldo who had no alibi to the contrary. He was at the crime scene within seconds, almost in the moment as, Ben's and Michael's arrival, gun poised ready to fire as Meryl arrived at the scene. When questioned, a Pandora's Box of bitter resentment against Andrei opened, hence his constant surveillance whenever Andrei was in Florence or when he hosted social gatherings at his home in Viareggio. His closeness to Boris Malakov revealed that he was on Boris' payroll, *a cash in hand* payment deal to investigate Andrei's connection to the media and other publication companies. This bit of information became evident when a once only electronic payment was made into his bank account from the shoe business in Russia. He had received large payments in cash each time Boris was in Florence. This 'arrangement' by a man who held unquestioned authority in the police department went undetected for five years.

Dmitri and Ana were subjected to the demands of Inspector Aldo to report to him on Andrei's movements while he was in Florence. Shocking information was revealed on the inspector's lascivious nature. The smooth-talking inspector was responsible for untold sexual harassment of Ana who despite her strong, impersonal exterior was a victim of his abuse over many years. His position as inspector was used to engender fear in Ana who wanted the best for her stepbrother, Boris. The inspector knew her weakness, he used her as housekeeper, spy and sex slave. He detested Andrei all the more based on his unfounded belief that Ana was his mistress. The charges against him grew in repulsive depth and breadth of what he was capable of and what he had committed. The media he once manipulated, was now bringing down his wall, tearing his reputation to shreds — headlines blared, *Salacious, Exploitation,* and *Sexual Predator* daily. Several anonymous telephone calls were received from wealthy, widowed women across Florence alleging he had sexually abused them under the guise of protection from gangs and thieves. He was responsible for ensuring Dmitri withheld information on Meryl's kidnapping. Inspector Aldo was with Dmitri the night Meryl was taken. He was in the car, under-cover of darkness, watching and waiting while safeguarding Boris' invasion of the picturesque villa beside the olive grove. Inspector Aldo and Dmitri were accomplices in the crime against Meryl; Dmitri it was accepted, was under duress from the inspector to do so.

That morning, in a packed-to-capacity courthouse with media mongrels sniffing on the prowl to be the first to spread the dirt, the judge addressed Inspector Aldo.

'Inspector Aldo, I now need to strip you of your 'Inspector' title. It aggrieves me that you have desecrated the responsibility and trust you have been given as one who had the privilege to uphold law and order in protecting the citizens of Florence. You conducted yourself without due diligence. What you have done is not only criminal but also immoral on *so many* grounds. I am going to outline these to you for your contemplation and rectification of your erroneous transgressions.'

The judge looked Aldo in the eye as he uttered these words like one who had rehearsed his lines, not looking once at his notes.

Aldo stood, arms taut, in erect stance with pursed lips and a defiant glare at the judge. He lapped up the 'attention' like a peacock's last-ditch effort to hang onto its plucked plume.

'Number one: you manipulated the power vested in you to serve your own ends in your criminal misdemeanours, this makes you the worst form of humanity that has been entrusted to uphold law and order in this land.

Number two: you bullied individuals, particularly, Dmitri Repin and Ana Kuznetsov... in cahoots with Boris Malakov in a travesty of justice, a complete and utter abuse of position.

Number three: you aided and abetted the abduction of Ms Meryl Moorecroft, a visitor, a foreigner and an upstanding individual, to our country.

Number four: you colluded with Francoise Dupain, a French national in extorting a sizable ransom for the abduction of Ms Moorecroft.

Number five: you harboured and concealed your interactions with two of Ms Moorecroft's kidnappers *while* the investigation was underway.

Number six: you expected and demanded sexual favours from Ms Kusnetsov while treating her like she was your possession, demanding that she takes care of your domestic chores.

Number seven: you manipulated the media in reporting only your version of the case on hand.

Number eight: you crafted threatening letters to Ms Moorecroft while the trial was in session which makes you a desensitized, debased, self-serving, narcissistic individual who will try anything to achieve your own ends.

Number nine: you purchased a firearm through a supplier in the UK which you neglected to register with the State Police Office.

You have abused the country of your birth along with its citizens in the tax payer's funding of this long drawn out investigation and trial.

Lying under oath regarding the role you played in the ongoing, persecution and final shooting of Professor Malakov has resulted in a sentence of fifteen years in prison to contemplate all your actions as outlined here today, in the fervent hope that you will be an older, dare I say, *wiser* or a better human being when you leave prison, which is not going to be an easy place for you, where many people know you as the bully, manipulator and reason why some of them are behind bars today.

You threatened Dmitri Repin and Ana Kusnetsov into refusing legal counsel when they were brought into custody. It is now obvious that you were threatened by being exposed if they had legal support.

The sexual harassment allegations that have since arisen from many women around the city will be tried in another sitting of this court.

I am not going to ask you for a response nor how you plead, you are **GUILTY** beyond every shadow of doubt.

'*Balivo!* Remove this man from my courtroom!'

*   *   *

Boris was to serve a five-year sentence for initiating and expediting the events that led to Meryl's abduction. The judge declared that while he did not shoot Andrei, he had orchestrated the entire operation to completion. He maintained he did not demand a ransom for Meryl's release. He denied knowing Francoise Dupain's whereabouts. He did not challenge the sentence which made Alec wonder what Boris was up to, his lack of resistance to a long prison sentence was completely out of character. It left Alec with an eerie feeling that if he was not going down kicking and screaming in his customary way, he must have something up his sleeve.

This disturbed Alec who was equally unnerved by Boris' lack of concern and grief over their mother's passing.

Dmitri Repin, for his part, was given a three year sentence, reduced to eighteen months when in the final moments he revealed that Inspector Aldo had far more to do with the matter outside his capacity of investigator. The judge deemed that he had every opportunity to report Inspector Aldo from the outset which he chose not to do. Ana was given eighteen months for being Boris' accomplice during the time Meryl was held in the remote outskirts of Florence. Once her sentence was served, Ana was denied further residency in Italy. She would have to return to Russia within forty-eight hours of her release. Meryl knew that Ana had a will of steel, she would meet out the entire eighteen months with stoic resolve for an earlier dismissal. She would comply in any way to prevent any further discrediting of Boris that would lead to a lengthening of his time in prison.

Meryl was baffled by such misguided allegiance.

Justice was served, Salvatore Aldo, stripped of his title was safely removed from society after being publicly disgraced for abusing his position. Meryl pondered what the late night news and morning newspaper headlines would reveal on their *Inspector Aldo!* She knew many more rats would emerge from his sinking ship, some of them being from the media corp.

A blog on these headlines burned deep within her!

*   *   *

Andrei was briefed on the final sentencing announcements.

He was satisfied that the law was just, for once.

'It's a wise move to let Ana return to Russia, I won't have her in my employ anymore and she will not be able to secure work here after all that has happened. She has no referees apart from me. She led a very insular life and that is clearly, as we now know, because she had so much to hide regarding Boris' antics and the despicable Aldo's abuse of her. I feel responsible for what she must have endured by bringing her to this country and leaving her for months at a time on her own. Her loyalty to Boris is admirable in this bizarre situation.'

'She was the ice maiden throughout the sentencing, a very difficult woman to read, I must say. You have no reason to feel guilty for the choices she made in life Andrei, you gave her an opportunity to become a self-made woman which she abused.' Meryl added.

'Yes indeed, she is a woman with dark secrets hence her tacit nature. I hope so *Merryl*, one never knows what problems might come when you lift someone from the quagmire of their lives. It has been a lesson for me, but will not deter me from helping those in need, I will have to lean on you *Merryl* for your intuition on this.'

'Dmitri sold Aldo's soul to the devil which certainly helped seal the suspicion that shrouded that diabolical man! Honour among thieves indeed!' Ben detested Aldo more so than ever after learning of his despicable sexual exploits and sickening, condescending harassment of Meryl.

'Dimitri Repin,' Andrei said with a faint smile, 'who would have thought he was involved at all, he was happy with his little taxi business and was reliable, I must give him due credit for turning up, on time, every time, I needed him. Will he have to return to Russia too after he serves his prison time?'

'No strangely, he seemed to have gained some kudos with the judge for spilling the beans on Aldo, I think.' Alec piped in.

'I certainly won't have him in my employ anymore either, he can keep the taxi business I bought for him all those years ago. He won't have much here now. Italians never forget injustice or inhumanity, they are loyal to each other as they are to family.

Dmitri is an outsider who was given the courtesy of acceptance, he has lost it now as a result of his own stupidity. No more *mi casa su casa*. The media is ruthless, they will keep the sordid memory alive. We have to put this to rest, I think a celebratory drink is in order!' Andrei surprised all with this suggestion.

'That won't be possible Andrei, I'm sure it's against hospital regulations and you certainly should not have any alcohol in your blood with all the meds you're on.' Ben raised a worried eyebrow.

'Doctor Spartan said a little glass of red was allowed, I spoke to my contacts within the hospital hierarchy.' Andrei laughed. 'Please ring for help *Merryl*.'

On cue, two catering staff emerged with a bottle of champagne and a bottle of red wine. A sealed glass with a straw inserted was on the tray, along with other wine glasses, to allow Andrei to have a sip or two of wine with Meryl assisting the glass to his lips.

Andrei was returning to her, his personality as she remembered from her brief time with him before the accident, was warm and fun-loving and thankfully alive and well.

Chapter 29

~

Andrei's physical recovery had not progressed as expected although his mind was agile and memory vibrant. Doctor Spartan suggested more surgery which Andrei vehemently rejected.

He was just happy to be alive.

Ben returned to London.

Meryl travelled between London and Florence to spend time with both Ben and Andrei. Andrei had taken up permanent residence in the villa in Viareggio, rarely commuting to the city. Ben had somewhat overcome his dread of air travel making fortnightly trips to Florence, spending a week at a time at the villa.

*   *   *

Writing Ben's biography excited Meryl while reigniting her curiosity regarding her own family origins.

Doctor Benvolio Hart was a man of great courage, conviction and compassion. He arrived in London as a student, a curious and eager eighteen year old. His parents wanted him to have a British education, nothing could convince them otherwise. He laughed whenever he remembered his mother's dissatisfaction with his teenage love interest. She was pleased, he said, to have him 'out of the girl's clutches.' He referred to his mother simply as 'Mother.' He had great admiration for her, saying she was a stoic woman with an unmovable will and physical strength to match. She gave her children a values-based upbringing, putting the needs of others first, surrendering to the will of God, conducting oneself with dignity and decorum at all times was a non-negotiable expectation. He fondly remembered that she detested loud, raucous laughter. He was often chastised for laughing without restraint. Meryl enjoyed the many days of recording and writing Ben's memories which became indelibly sewn into her soul.

'I remember Mother being annoyed with a lady, a Mrs Nagar, if I remember correctly, who laughed she said, 'like a launching spaceship,' why 'spaceship?' is a question I did not clarify or more like dared not clarify. Mother's actual words were, 'she lacks any decency, a very shameful display of poor manners indeed!' Ben laughed like a mischievous boy for whom the moment relived, elicited fond emotions. He said Mother had large gatherings at the house and even though they were a suitably well-off family, she did not discriminate between the domestic staff and family like other families did in the day. She had a passion for music and the arts and read with great zeal. He lovingly credited his mother for instilling his passion for literature. He also referred to his father as 'Father' who he said was very preoccupied with the business so Mother kept the home fires burning. His father knew that his mother was a strong, capable woman who did not need a man to run her life. She was proudly feminist back in the late 1920's although raucous laughter, especially from a woman was taboo in her book!

'What were your school days like Ben? Did you go to a co-educational school or was it a boys' school?'

With a cheeky twinkle in his eye, Ben continued to narrate his boyhood days. 'I went to a co-educational school, that's where I met Susan, in junior high school. We were sweethearts from the first day we met and it was impossible to hide, we tried to grab every minute we could to be with each other. Mother was livid, especially when her suspicions were confirmed when she found a poem I had written to Susan. I will never forget what she said in a bid to make my blood run cold to end the relationship, all she said was, 'Remember what happened to Romeo and Juliet? Remember that Ben.'

'You were quite young, that threat should have made your blood run cold. How is it that you were not afraid?'

'I knew Mother was strict in her expectations of us, her children, she was equally forgiving, but she did not like Susan because she was Mrs Nagar's niece! She might have been concerned that our decorous lifestyle would be shattered by loud, 'spaceship' peals of laughter!' Ben laughed as tears rolled down his, now, very lean face. Meryl relished the mirth that gushed forth during each session of her research into Ben's life. She knew much about him but these hidden gems brought many hours of light-heartedness which they had both missed during the dark days of Andrei's time in hospital. Many late nights were spent sitting in the lounge room with Meryl either audio recording Ben or tapping at great speed on her laptop as he reminisced about his life across time and space, drawing Meryl in to all the intimate and intricate details of a young man's life during his era.

Ben recalled arriving in London alone and having to fend for himself, after having a mother who doted on her children. A rather reserved Ben, withdrew into his world of books, study and later work life. He rose to the pinnacle of his field, giving lectures to medical students, making extensive contributions to medical journals and treating a few celebrities along the way. After fifty years in London, he was glad he accepted his mother's decision to have him shipped off, away from Susan.

'Did you communicate with Susan while you were here in the early days? It would have probably been through telegrams and letter writing, I suppose.'

'Ahem! Yes, at my age that would have been the mode of communication but alas we never met again nor communicated after I left. I expect if I had not made that move, I would not have advanced in my career, there were not many opportunities back in the day in the old country; I might have become a teacher or a writer, who knows. My other passion rests firmly there too. I enjoyed medical teaching, you know but by night I read and re-read the classics.'

'For which I am truly grateful, your influence has impacted on my life greatly on that score!'

Meryl's blogs had become very popular in the past two years, she wrote inspirational pieces on healing from injury and how an active mind was beneficial to an aging body. She wrote from an earthy, reliable voice and had many offers to speak at local charity lunches and dinners which she found difficult to decline even when she had a jam-packed visit in London. Her life was busy with commuting between Viareggio and London and writing the books she had long yearned to write. The space she craved was granted albeit a hectic lifestyle of flitting between the many hats she now wore. This was a life she would not trade for any other.

Ben had great difficulty accepting praise or value for what he had done or continued to do for others. He often changed the subject to other areas of his life. His humility always touched her, a quality she hoped she could emulate.

'You asked about my school days and I wafted off about my infatuation with Susan! I am really happy that you have Andrei in your life, Meryl, it's so important to have a like-minded partner. I really don't believe that jazz about how opposites attract and I realised that as I matured. Had it not been for Mother's interference, I would have been quite miserable with Susan. I would quote love poems to her but they were lost on her, she did not have the privilege, I had, growing up with books, we had a library in our home, a very large one too. I spent many happy hours reading *Anna Karenina, Crime and Punishment,* all of Charles Dickens' novels and *The Complete Works of William Shakespeare.* You would have loved my childhood home, especially the library with its Victorian ambience. Teachers were dedicated to promoting reading, we had a quota of books that we had read placed on the leader board, the competition was fierce, I tell you, to get to the top of the reading leader board! Many book club nights and drama nights filled my teenage days. We lived in an age of no television, well no technology at all, in the old country, so there were no distractions to deter us from these cultured events. For that, I am eternally grateful. I was an armchair traveller from the day I could read.'

'Yes, we should not take for granted being raised in a literary family, Grandma Beth was an avid reader which had a great impact on my father who loved reading. His busy life kept him away from family duty but he ensured I had a stack of books, most of them based on your recommendations, to keep me busy and out of trouble!'

'My childhood was a marvellous one Meryl. Good old-school

values which has kept me strong. Books, music and the theatre have been significant in my life as they are in yours, nothing can replace any of those — Twitter, Facebook and all the other social media sites that have their value in our world today, which generates at the speed of light but cannot replace watching live players on a stage or reading into the lives of characters with a book in hand that a playwright or author has carefully crafted, pouring heart and soul into their creations. I know you love blogging now and that you create mini narratives with each one, it's a quick read in this fast-paced world, I have not quite come to terms with the brevity that people crave as they dash through life, flitting from one thing to another. Young people must learn to stop and smell the roses again or as they might say *the coffee!* Or perhaps that expression has become obsolete since I last looked!' He laughed at his musings on the state of the world adding in that he was getting too old for any more change.

'Oh Ben, don't get morose on me now, I know you to be the oldest man as far as numbers go but that you are the person who speaks to my understanding of the world as no other person can... stop smiling, I know what you're thinking, *what about the 'roving professor' Meryl?*' she laughed. 'Not even Andrei comes close to my understanding of the world that you have given me, so there! 'Getting too old for any change,' to put it the only way I can, in true Ben style is, 'what a load of bunkum sir!'

'Dear me, Meryl, I have created you in my own image, that's a worrisome thought!' he laughed again making Meryl feel carefree as always in his company. If there was one thing she knew of Ben, it was that he never judged anyone until they gave him very good reason to do so.

He had formed a close relationship with Andrei, now that he understood that he was a man of great virtue, a man who would add to the gifts that Meryl already possessed. He believed they were a formidable duo that would contribute much to art, literature and culture of the day. He believed that greatness was a birthright that could flourish in well-chosen relationships, Meryl enhanced his greatness, as family who loved without conditions, without expectations, just happy to be alive, and together in good times and in need. He knew Andrei would watch and celebrate Meryl's further growth and contributions to the world.

Ben explained that his early days as a medical man were not well received by some of his peers, the stalwarts of the medical board who could not see beyond his skin tone. His retreat into the literary world was to block out the memory of this struggle in a country he loved as his mother's chosen homeland for him. It took persistence, lonely nights and amazing breakthrough research before he was somewhat accepted by some, not by all, he made a note of including, into the medical fold.

The message he left Meryl lingered with timeless resonance.

Colonialism had its way with making us believe we were inadequate, if we mimicked the lifestyle and values it upheld, we were embraced with open arms. Nobody said we would remain the outsider for the rest of our coloured days. We have to be true to who we are, warts, skin colour and all, we must acknowledge our birthright, our roots, let no one take that from you if you are to lead an authentic life which will keep you whole and bring you peace.

Chapter 30

Doubt thou the stars are fire;
Doubt that the sun doth move;
Doubt truth to be a liar;
But never doubt I love.
Shakespeare — Hamlet

~

M eryl was always restless before a big event. She last dreamt of her mother when she was in London, the night she experienced what she thought, then, was a sudden *dark side* to Professor Andrei Malakov, the night he had a harsh telephone conversation on the way to *The Phantom of the Opera*.

*　　*　　*

She was an adult, at her current age, walking along a sunset beach, seagulls swooping overhead in large circles and dives. The distinct horn of a ship approaching was heard in the distance — a slow, sonorous horn like that from another world. Beside her, walked her mother, untouched by time, smiling at her, bathed in a sea of sparkling light. 'You've done well Meryl, I'm so proud of you. You have much to look forward to. Our needs change as we pass through life, mature and age. I'm here beside you, you will know my signs to you, remember that across time and space, in good times and not so good times, I'll always be here.' With the last sound of the horn, she was gone, nodding and smiling as she wafted out of view.

*　　*　　*

Today marked two years since that fateful day of Andrei's shooting.

Meryl stood in the glare of the academic spotlight at Oxford University. She fantasised as a teenager that she would deliver an unforgettable talk on this very stage. She looked up at the packed to capacity auditorium, this moment was surreal, here she was realising the dreams of her young adult life.

'Good evening respected Dean and academic staff of the English department, ladies and gentlemen. It is with great honour, this evening that I present Professor Andrei Malakov who has been absent from the literary limelight for some time as you know. The media left no stone unturned and have turned a few imaginary stones too,' she looked up smiling, many heads nodded in the audience in acknowledgement of the gutter press on Andrei's shooting two years earlier, surmising and speculating the worst-case scenarios.

'Professor Malakov, while in recovery and rehabilitation before he could return to his literary public life has been fruitfully engaged during this period of seclusion.'

'You will be happy to know, first up, that his much-anticipated biography on William Shakespeare which unveils information, never before available to the public eye, will be out in March this year. While recuperating, Professor Malakov continued to work on the biography he promised the world, *Shakespeare, A*

Friend and Mentor which will be available here at the university library and across the globe, I'm pleased to announce.'

The audience applauded. Meryl stood, undaunted, confident as she had never been before in public let alone academic forums. Ben sat smiling in the front row, directly in Meryl's line of vision. With deep respect, she acknowledged that she was infinitely blessed to still have Ben in her life — in this moment where she held her own — strong — confident and ready to take on the world. She knew she would not have come this far, had it not been for his belief in her, supporting her through her self-doubts, failures and significant life decisions.

Alec and Brad sat next to Ben, like close family would during memorable moments in each other's lives. They were now married and proud, doting parents of adopted twins. Each one, Ben, Alec, Brad, Andrei and Meryl had become stronger and closer. Andrei's crisis forged this formidable connection, a bond closer than most families could boast.

Meryl looked up at the audience, glowing as she went on,

'I'm most delighted to now call upon Professor Malakov to address you.'

She stood back, smiling, waiting. Life in recent months had taught her patience.

All eyes turned to the right of the stage as Professor Andrei Malakov, dressed to perfection, in a charcoal-grey suit, white shirt, black cravat and a smile that encircled his bright curious eyes, fixed his gaze on Meryl.

He rode in on his motorised wheelchair with the aura of a crown prince on his celestial carriage, delighted to be back home to his people, where he belonged.

A thunderous almost unending applause rose up to the rafters of the auditorium ringing out in an ovation celebrating his return to the academic fold.

Andrei remained, smiling and composed. It was an older Andrei that looked up at his audience, wiser after his brush with death in matters of the heart and soul.

'Thank you, ladies and gentlemen, what a privilege to be back with you here tonight. A moment, I thought I would never relive during my days of recovery. Where there is a will, there most certainly is a way with supportive, caring people around you.' He looked across at Meryl who sat on a seat to the left of him and down to Ben, Alec and Brad and continued.

'Tonight's talk is not solely a literary one, it is largely an inspirational one which will take you into my private world, which I am now at liberty to share. Life has its cavernous twists and turns to make us aware that we have much to offer, even in our darkest moments, when we struggle to make it through to the next day, when we need assistance to sip a drink of water, we have something valuable to offer others. Poor choices in young adult life threw me many challenges. The thing that kept me on solid ground was my love for my son Alec, and the world of reading, studying and giving back to eager young minds. That sustained me through my days of poor judgement made as a young man and again when my life was threatened by the trauma of having a bullet lodged in my skull. What were the chances of me ever speaking, thinking, learning, reading and studying again? Pretty slim is what my doctor tells me today. It was thought I would remain on life support and remain a vegetable for the rest of my days. Two voices kept me going when I was floating in the nether realm, neither here nor dead, in eternal limbo. All the beautiful poetry on life and loss did not prepare me for that thin line which separates life from death. The relentless conversations from two people who are here with me tonight kept me alive by wanting me to return to them. I heard them but could not reply. I felt their pain and heard their quiet concerns when they thought I was not listening. I was in a powerful position, so loved and cared for and privy to secret conversations without being found out!' The audience laughed.

Andrei's sense of humour was intact and stronger now, he was no longer serious about life and himself, he took each day as it came, giving thanks that he was here to see another rising of the sun. 'We cannot go through life alone, we are *not* meant to. We have a collective purpose.'

The resounding applause fuelled his soul.

"Thank you,' are two simple words from one who respects life with greater care and value these days. Remember, you have much to offer, let nothing stop you from making a difference.

I will now move on to the release of my biography on William Shakespeare.'

Andrei spoke for an hour without showing signs of fatigue, enjoying that he could share his passionate life's work, his research, his favourite plays and poems that he exulted and glorified. He brought Shakespeare back to life that night.

Ben sat listening in awe of the *roving professor* at whom he looked with a dubious eye, two years ago. Meryl was destined to be with him, in this moment and forevermore. Meryl, the lost girl he felt so close to was now a woman shining in her own light. He was proud to see her emerge from the trauma of the past two years to a courageous woman with a firm mission.

'I have given my ultimate and respectful nod to William Shakespeare, a contribution to his life and works that I felt compelled to do, to celebrate the meaning and understanding of life in my darkest moments. Many have done this before me, with tremendous success in elevating the timeless connection to the life and times of William Shakespeare. I wanted to bring you, Shakespeare the man as I have come to respect him, I hope you find it refreshing, I hope you find something new that will be an 'aha' moment for you as many such moments I encountered during my research,' he said, pausing as he absorbed the passion surging within.

'Before I close tonight, I would like to introduce Ms Moorecroft who is assisting me with the writing of my autobiography, on her insistence I might add, that I should document my life, my answer to her was that only a remarkable life need be documented and many such conversations led to her convincing me that I should go ahead with it,' he looked at Meryl smiling in gratitude of her belief in him.

'I take this moment, if you will indulge me in giving you a significant look into my autobiography right here, right now, a 'pre-publication verbal release,' as it were, the part of my life that I am so proud of.' His voice sounded tight, caught in his throat for a second.

'I give thanks for what I'm about to reveal in the words of my eternal master, William Shakespeare,

O Lord that lends me life, Lend me a heart replete with thankfulness (Henry V1, part 2)

Meryl looked at Andrei, unsure of how much he was about to reveal, she knew him to be a very private man, it took much coercion and a bit of pressure coupled with her feminine charm to get him to concede to co-writing his autobiography. She sucked in her breath and waited.

'Ladies and gentlemen, it gives me such great joy... that I know I will always have, each time I introduce *Mrs Merryl Malakov,* my beloved, *moya zvezda,* my wife, my scribe, my new life.' If only he could hold out his arms, he would call her into his embrace.

A rapturous applause followed by another standing ovation that evening, made Meryl feel very self-conscious, all eyes were on her. Blood rushed to her face. She thanked her lucky stars that her dark skin concealed her flushed face as her heart thundered in jubilation of this moment she had dreamt of as a young girl.

Time stood still as a sea of smiling faces shared in the joy of this very public announcement by a very private man.

Ben and Alec walked up to the stage to share this moment with Professor Andrei and Mrs Meryl Malakov.

Meryl looked down at Andrei, nothing could make her more complete than a show of such profound love. She was publicly acknowledged as the wife of a man she was fated to spend the rest of her the days with – he shared her passion for literature and writing – he did not question her motivations and passion in the choices she made to serve her purpose to herself and others.

Meryl looked above the audience, she felt the glow of her mother's presence bathed in a haze of sparkling light, smiling down at her, hands clasped in blissful reverence — she had found her place in the world.

~

The valiant never taste of death but once.
Shakespeare — Julius Caesar

Also by Mala Naidoo

Would you risk your long held dreams for a secluded estate beside an olive grove, a creative paradise, and a mysterious, irresistible newcomer? Set in London and Florence with a third location being 'any place' Meryl, a budding writer, and Michael a human rights lawyer, become entangled in the world of international crime. Life will never be quite the same. Will they pick up from where they left, despite the various characters who managed to enter their lives, or will they let go of the safety they once found in each other's arms?

A contemporary story of fractured pasts, intriguing encounters, insularity, professional harassment and the capacity to live for others.

Published by Sid Harta Publishers.

www.ingramcontent.com/pod-product-compliance
Lightning Source LLC
Chambersburg PA
CBHW030646110726
47901CB00002B/592